# The Opening Door

*I was alone, dreadfully alone, in the threatening house. All that there was of evil lay below me in the dark hall-way.*

*I heard the tread of feet on the carpeted steps, measured and relentless as doom. My legs stiff with fear, I moved toward safety, my fingers groping for the catch. The door slid open, I fell inside, and closed the door of my secret room, my sanctuary.*

*It seemed a figment of my terror when a moment later I heard the panel move, and felt chill air caress my icy skin. It was against all reason, yet someone had opened the door to my hidden room, and was moving toward me. . . .*

# HEATHER

**Maeva Park Dobner**

A DELL BOOK

Published by

DELL PUBLISHING CO., INC.

750 Third Avenue

New York, New York 10017

Dell ® TM 681510, Dell Publishing Co., Inc.

Printed in the United States of America

First printing—September 1970

*"For my mother"*

# HEATHER

# 1

*How easily murder is discovered.*
—SHAKESPEARE

The house was like a jewel. I possessed it as though it were my own, and not, in fact, Miss Grimes's tiny house with the secret room beside the stair.

On that autumn night when things began to change, to shift and move about, to take on new shapes, I had been living at 1 Greenwood Place for nearly five months, and I had achieved an odd sort of happiness, a kind of wary belief that life might be good again.

That evening I sat reading quietly in the Victorian sitting room, with its burgundy-velvet draperies, its shabby, graceful love seat, half-listening to the rain drumming upon the windowpane. From time to time, I spread my hands to the glowing gas log in the brown-marble fireplace and let the warmth seep into my bones, for it seemed to me that I was always cold, that I had been frozen ever since the night Jed had gone.

I heard Louise clicking down the stairs. She came and stood in the sitting-room doorway, a slender girl in a belted white raincoat, with a half-dozen books under one arm; a young woman about my own age, with a short, square face and square white teeth. In repose, her mouth was disciplined, almost prim, but when she talked, quickly and dramatically, her face came to vivid, magnetic life. It did so now, when she spoke the most prosaic of words.

"I'm just going to walk up to the branch library with

these," she said. "They're overdue."

"It's raining," I told her dubiously. "Why don't you drive?"

"I don't mind. I need the fresh air." She put the hood of her coat over her bright hair. "It's too much trouble to go across the street and get the car out of the garage."

She started toward the little entry hall, then turned around with an afterthought. "Sydney, Felix called me tonight. He wanted to know if you'd like to go out with us Wednesday night. He has a friend he's sure you'll like. And I'll be playing at the Ferris Wheel the rest of the week, you know, so it's the only chance I'll have for a night on the town."

I smiled politely, noncommittally. "No," I said. "Thank you, but no, not just now."

She shrugged. "Well, suit yourself, but you're letting life run away from you. Eat, drink, and be merry, you know."

She turned, with a little flip of the hand, and went from the softly lighted room. I heard the front door open, then shake the house with its closing, and then the sound of her going was lost in the beat of the rain.

I picked up my book, but it was a long time before I began to read again. Was I being foolish, I wondered, shutting myself off from life because of the bitter memory of Jed? Louise knew nothing of my brief marriage, yet I sometimes had the feeling that she sensed my problem and wanted to help. It was her nervous, energetic way to take action, to move, to do things, while I, more introspective and more careful, hesitated before moving.

It came to me then that I knew as little of Louise as she did of me. Her friends? That evanescent, ever-changing, potpourri of musicians, socialites, newspapermen, young doctors and lawyers—I had met many of them, but actually, what did they tell of Louise herself? Only that she was fascinating, in her own self-contained way, and that she knew a great many people: Cecily, Felix, Lucien, Irene, Phil. . . .

I stirred restlessly and looked at the clock. Only nine-thirty, but the fire's warmth and the rain's rhythm had combined to make me sleepy.

"Come on, then," I said to Thomas, the seven-toed yellow cat, who was perched in his favorite place atop the television set. "Let's go to bed."

The library, no more than fifteen minutes' walk from the house, closed at nine, and I decided Louise must have met someone she knew and stopped for coffee, as she often did. To me she seemed frenetically social, wanting people about her all the time.

I went up the thinly carpeted stairway, the cat draped over my shoulder. At the landing, beside the small, hidden room, I paused for a moment and let my fingers slide over the catch at the side of the big mirror. On the day she had rented the house to me, Miss Grimes had showed me the secret room, as a sign of special favor, and I had revealed it later to Louise; but no one else had seen it. It was wonderfully private and secluded.

I loved the little room. In those first hard weeks, after Jed, my husband, had gone, and I had come away from sorrow to a new life in a new city, I had thought often of Miss Grimes's secret room. It had seemed to offer me that sanctuary which it had given to groups of runaway slaves from the South, back in the Civil War days.

Sometimes I would go and sit there idly in the stillness and peace, and think of the tired and frightened people with their brown-velvet faces and their bewildered dark eyes, and I would count myself lucky. Lucky, lucky, lucky—and then the bitterness would set in, and the slow, burning anger because I, with honesty and forthrightness as my birthright, had been taken in deceit.

I went on upstairs and deposited Thomas on my bed. He uttered a little chirp of pleasure, then proceeded to give himself a complete bath, his small pink tongue working vigorously, his amber eyes narrowed in absorption. I watched him as though mesmerized. He was all I had to love, and I loved him. At last he began a series of turnings, making small, futile circles, and presently settled, purring, on the comforter.

I opened the window, and the scent of rain-washed earth

and wet leaves rushed into the room. The downpour was steady, splashing noisily on the slate roof, rushing gurgling through the gutters. I loved the rain, but tonight it had a lonely sound, forcing me to remember the feeling of strong young arms about my waist, the sight of bold green eyes laughing into mine, the touch of firm, smooth lips on my own.

Like the rain, the tears coursed down my cheeks, and I let myself give way to grief, as I had not given way in all the weeks in San Francisco. In that little restaurant on Fisherman's Wharf, with its unforgettable smell of lobster pots and with the pearly pink seashells in the window—there I had not cried, as I watched Jed walk away. Not then, nor since.

But here at last, here in the peace and quietude of my small sanctuary, I let sorrow and desolation have their way with me. For a long time I looked out at the dark garden, not understanding the renewed sense of loss which I had tonight, the same lonely feeling I'd experienced as a child, when I'd opened the door on a cold night and felt myself solitary in the world.

I shook off the feeling finally, turned off the lamp, and climbed into bed, grateful for the purring, living presence of Thomas.

My dreams were a jumble of Jed, and that little motel in Santa Monica, and the Ferris Wheel, and the electric typewriter in the Hoffman Conservatory, where I worked, and something dark and frightening which lurked in the little room beside the stair.

I awoke to the jangling cry of the doorbell. Someone was leaning on the bell; it pealed wildly through the little house. I struggled into my robe, switched on the hall light, and hurried, still hazy with sleep, down the narrow staircase.

The broad-shouldered man who stood there, in the dark of the porch, was elegantly tall, elegantly dressed, and I thought at first that he was drunk. He leaned on the door frame as though he could not quite support himself.

"Miss Webster?"

"Yes?"

I saw his face then, a ravaged mask of grief, and I recognized him dimly as the man whose portrait sat on Louise's dresser. "That's Domenic Lawrence," she had said once, when I had commented on the square, firm-jawed face, the direct, uncompromising gaze. "He's a good friend. You'll meet him eventually. He's in Ireland now, on some sort of inheritance case for one of his clients. He's an attorney."

At the time, I had thought there was a betraying hint of affection in her quick, controlled voice, and certainly there was some significance in the very presence of his photograph on her dresser; but I had never met him.

"Louise," he said now, this man in the portrait, "Louise is dead."

Perhaps knowing Jed had conditioned me to violence, or perhaps it was only that I was still dazed with sleep. I only know that it didn't occur to me that Louise had died from natural causes.

I swayed a little, standing there in the dimly lit entrance hall, and I said, in a curious, feeble voice, "How was she killed?"

# 2

Centennial Park was only a few blocks from Greenwood
Place, and Domenic Lawrence and I were there within
twenty minutes from the time he'd appeared at my door. I
had hurried back upstairs, thrown on a sweater and skirt,
and rejoined him, and we had ridden almost wordlessly
toward the little park.

The night was quiet, the city park deserted, for a rainy
autumn evening is too damp, too lonely, to lure lovers into
its chill embrace. A yellow, vaporous fog, clinging to the
streetlamps, cast a sort of malevolence over the stretch of
wooded area through which we were riding.

We drew up sharply and stopped with a screech of brakes.
On a little curved cement bridge they were gathered: policemen in yellow slickers, plainclothesmen in belted raincoats,
photographers—a swarm of men, hovering over the quiet
body in the white raincoat. To one side stood a young man
and a girl, the two who had found Louise, I assumed. They
huddled unnoticed in the rain.

"Come on," said Domenic Lawrence dully. "I think they'll
want you to identify her."

I looked at him in swift, instinctive protest, and he said
flatly, "I can't."

Two words, and I knew he'd loved Louise.

He hadn't mentioned this on the way over. His few words
had been quiet and factual. "I was driving in from New
York," he'd said, "and I heard the police call on my car
radio. A young couple, walking home through the park after
a movie, found her. The police said her name was Louise

Albright; they'd found identification in her wallet. I couldn't take it in, not then. I called Captain Morley of homicide, who's a friend of mine, and he told me to get you and come here."

As though in a dream, I got out of the car and walked toward the tableau on the bridge. It was Louise, sprawled stiff-legged, like a doll, upon the wet grass and leaves. Her bright hair had escaped its barrette and spilled onto the ground, its softness lighted theatrically by the whirring beacon on the news car.

As I knelt there in the mud, with the mist curling about my head, I thought of Louise as she had been, alive. She had come to the house on Greenwood Place one wet Sunday in late summer; my first sight of her, like this, my last, had been in the rain. She'd stood there on the doorstep, in this same expensive raincoat, and I remember being impressed by the careless extravagance of her thin-heeled pumps, unprotected, even though the rain was teeming down upon the dark, slick pavement and rushing headlong into the gutters.

She'd answered my advertisement for someone to share the house, an ad I'd inserted reluctantly in the morning paper, only because the rent was really too much for me alone. I'd chosen Louise, from a line of young women, garrulous girls and imperious older women, because I'd felt sure that she wasn't the kind to infringe on my personal life.

"Well?" The police lieutenant's voice had a little edge of impatience.

I sat back upon my heels. "This is Louise Albright. She was my roommate. I cannot imagine what she was doing here. She'd set out for the library."

A raindrop, trembling on Louise's watch crystal, caught up the light and made a tiny rainbow on her wrist. I watched it, fascinated. The lieutenant put a gentle hand under my elbow and lifted me to my feet. "You'd better go sit in one of the cars," he said kindly. "It's pouring again."

"How did she die?" I asked, scarcely hearing him.

"She was shot from behind," he said shortly.

Someone led me toward one of the police cars, and a flash

bulb exploded in my face. For the first time, I felt something: fear and a little anger.

"Do I have to be photographed?" I demanded of the young policeman who was escorting me.

"We'll ask him not to use it," he said soothingly.

I sat shivering uncontrollably in the overheated car, and Domenic Lawrence got in beside me. Like two wretched strangers cast up on a desert island, we huddled together, sharing a common misery. It was plain enough that he was suffering the tortures of the damned over the death of the girl he loved, while I still shook over the memory of my friend lying on the wet dark leaves. So short a time ago, she'd been a living creature, going out the door with an armload of books whose pages still bore the faint impress of her fingers, the scent of her perfume.

"How did they find my name?" I asked Domenic Lawrence.

"Your name and mine were on an identification card in her purse," he said dully. "She had put us down as the persons to be called in case of accident."

Accident. "Shot from behind," the police lieutenant had said. That was murder, surely, but murder is something that happens to people in books, or possibly to someone on the other side of the city; but never on one's own street, never to a friend.

"All that vitality, all that life," he was muttering. It was as if he said to me, You were her friend, you must know how she was, how terrible is my loss.

He looked at me out of eyes dark with pain. "I used to love watching her drink a brandy," he said, "or tell a funny story. Why, just hearing her say, 'Hello, Domenic,' was exciting."

"I know," I said gently. I was beginning to come out of shock now, and I could feel compassion for him.

"Do you think they'd let us leave now?" I asked after a long interval of silence. "It's cruel of them to keep you sitting here."

I leaned out of the car window, and my eye was drawn

fatally to the lighted scene against the trees. They were putting her on a stretcher now, two men working busily and efficiently.

The young policeman came over to us. "The medical examiner is finished," he said. "I'll drive you home now, miss, if you like. We'll talk to you tomorrow, probably."

"No, no," said Domenic Lawrence impatiently. "I'll take her home."

We climbed out of the police car and watched in fascinated horror, unable to turn away, as they loaded the stretcher into the morgue wagon. I felt, rather than saw, the shudder go through Domenic Lawrence's tall, lean frame, as the two attendants slammed the door and fastened it.

Like a stage going dark after a performance, the spotlights were turned off the little patch of ground, the news wagon wheeled away, the policemen got into the waiting cars, and a hush began to settle over the park.

I followed Domenic Lawrence to his car, and we drove away in silence. There were a dozen questions I wanted to ask him, but his grim features were so forbidding that I sat there quietly, huddled into my corner. The penetrating dampness seemed to invade the very marrow of my bones, but he had forgotten to turn on the heater, and appeared oblivious of the chill air.

When he pulled up in front of the narrow little house on Greenwood Place, he suddenly seemed aware that I was there. A little frown appeared between his brows. "I hadn't realized you'd be spending the rest of the night alone," he said. "Shall I take you to a friend or relative?"

I shook my head. "Louise was the only friend I had in the city, and I've no relatives here. I'm from California."

He switched off the motor. "Then let me come in and sit with you. I don't think you should be alone. If Louise's murder was deliberate and not an accident or the work of a psychotic, then the murderer must be someone she knew."

I started to say stiffly that I was perfectly capable of taking care of myself. Then I realized that it was he who dared not be alone, that he could not endure the small, lonely hours of the early morning without some human companionship, even from a stranger.

"Well, come in then," I said, and started up the high stone steps.

It was a measure of my misery and fatigue that, when the key didn't turn at once in the old-fashioned lock, I nearly burst into tears.

"Take off your coat," I told him, when we were in the tiny vestibule. "I'll turn up the heat. I don't think I'll ever be warm again."

"For God's sake, find me a drink," he ordered, and went into the sitting room and flung his length into a chair.

I mixed very stiff whiskey-and-sodas, and we drained our glasses in silence. I made refills. Then we sat together, in the oddest sort of companionship, waiting for news, waiting for the phone to ring, waiting for morning.

Sometimes I drowsed a little, my head against the back of the blue wing chair. I thought idly of making coffee, of turning on the gas log, but the effort seemed too great. A sort of lassitude had taken possession of me, and the headache which had been threatening, earlier in the evening, had become a tight, painful reality.

Something brought me sharply awake, as my eyes roamed the high-ceiled sitting room, which might have been preserved, like Sleeping Beauty's castle, for a hundred years.

For a moment I couldn't put my finger on the reason for the faint uneasiness I felt, the little breath of fear. And then I knew. It was the china pug, which sat on the lowest shelf of the whatnot stand in the corner.

On the day I had rented the house, I had stood holding the dog in my hand, entranced by the delightful ugliness of it, when Miss Grimes had returned with the tea she had insisted upon giving me.

"That was my nephew's favorite piece," she'd said, startling me a little with her reappearance. Her long, narrow feet in their sensible black oxfords had made no sound on the well-preserved Brussels carpet.

I took the tea tray from her and placed it on a table.

"I am something of an amateur astrologer," she said, her hands busy with the tea things. "I worked out my nephew's horoscope long ago, and I know what his fate must be. He will come to a violent end."

I shivered in spite of myself. She sounded so sure.

She sighed, passing me my cup. "I loved the boy, but I've always felt rather glad I didn't marry and have children. One runs the risk of having one's child turn out like him. That's cowardly of me, of course. Don't let it influence you, my dear."

"I won't," I said, trying to smile.

She went on to tell me of a particularly malicious prank her nephew once had played on her: he had sent a friend to tell his aunt that he had fallen in the river, and in fact, his clothes had been found on the river bank; but all the time he was hiding in the secret room, waiting to laugh at her terror and her grief.

Well, Miss Grimes, retired from schoolteaching, was touring Europe now, and the bitter little story had nothing to do with tonight's tragedy. Still, I shivered forlornly in the quiet room, and it seemed to me that that long-ago malice had left its mark on the little house, and that I had been expecting tragedy all along.

The night spun itself out into dawn, and still we sat, Domenic Lawrence and I, keeping our silent vigil. The rain had stopped, and the pale sunlight crept in through the thin line between the red-velvet draperies, and rested on the ivory chessmen, and on the carved features of the man who sat, immobile, across from me.

It was the face of a man sailing a ship, his eyes fixed on the sea, his firm jaw jutting out; or a farmer, perhaps, in an earlier time, a rugged outdoor man, plowing a straight furrow, riding a horse across sun-swept fields. He was a man out of his time, an anachronism on a city street or at a country-club dance. But then I thought of the broad shoulders one day wearing a judge's robes, the strong face watching, weighing evidence, and I knew that Domenic Lawrence, in any age, was a man with whom one must reckon, a strong man, only temporarily laid low by grief.

Thomas, refreshed after a good night's sleep, came downstairs, stretching and yawning. He looked at me and meowed inquiringly, and finally I arose wearily and went with him to the kitchen.

I opened a can of cat food, and Thomas rubbed his head vigorously against my ankles, purring his accord with my actions. Then I measured coffee and water into the percolator, put cups on a tray, and let Thomas outdoors, before going back to switch on the radio in the sitting room.

As if coming back from a great distance, Domenic Lawrence leaned forward to listen. First the announcer gave the national news, and we waited tensely for him to get on.

Then came the local news, and the voice of the announcer, sounding excited and rushed and faintly exaggerated:

"Shortly after midnight last night, the body of a young woman was discovered in Centennial Park. She had been shot in the back, apparently by a .22-caliber bullet, according to police. The body was discovered by two students from the Hoffman Conservatory.

"The young woman has been identified as Louise Albright, of 1 Greenwood Place. Miss Albright had been doing graduate work at the conservatory. She was employed on weekends as pianist and singer at a local night club, the Ferris Wheel."

The announcer paused, and his voice took a deeper, more dramatic tone. "Felix Reichmann, an instructor at the conservatory, described as a close friend of Miss Albright, was brought in for questioning by the police only an hour ago. According to Detective Captain John C. Morley, Reichmann was seen with Miss Albright when she left the Sutton Avenue Branch Library at nine P.M."

I looked at Domenic Lawrence. He was white to the lips, and the tight anger on his face was terrifying. I suddenly realized that I was alone in the house with a man of whom I knew absolutely nothing.

"Who," he demanded, "is Felix Reichmann?"

I said weakly, "I thought—I think he was a boyfriend of sorts. A friend, anyway."

With visible effort he shook off his anger. "I had no strings on Louise, if that's what you're wondering." His voice changed. "But I think—I think I might have married her."

I went and got the coffee then, and we sat drinking it, each thinking our own dark thoughts. Suddenly I gave an exclamation of dismay, and splashed the hot, dark liquid on my wrist.

He looked at me wearily.

"I was just wondering if Louise had relatives who should be notified. She did tell me that she was alone in the world, since her aunt and uncle died, but surely there must be someone."

He got up, tall and dark-browed and remote, seeming to fill the room. "She had no one," he said. "Now, you'd better get some sleep, Miss Webster. The police will be sending for you later in the day, I imagine, to find out what you knew about Louise and her activities."

He walked toward the tiny foyer, and I followed him, feeling sick, feeling frightened, and hating the fact that I was feeling anything, after I had schooled myself so patiently to live only on the surface of life.

Domenic Lawrence seemed to rouse himself from some inner world to which he'd retreated. "By the way," he said, "I was Louise's attorney as well as her friend, you know. I shall probably have to come and see you in a day or two."

I felt a dull surprise at the idea that Louise had needed a lawyer, but I said merely, "Good-bye. Thank you for staying," and he went out.

After he had gone, I stood for a long time leaning on the cool glass of the window which formed the upper sash of the front door. For one who had been brought up happily and peacefully in a sun-swept parsonage in Monterey, I thought bitterly, I seemed to have a remarkable facility for choosing associates who brought me in contact with the police.

## 3

*Most musical of mourners, weep again!*
                                      —SHELLEY

The police were nice enough, after all. I went in to headquarters in the afternoon, when they sent for me, and told Captain Morley every tiny detail of the evening before. He was very polite; they were all very polite. I didn't think any of them believed that I had streaked the seven blocks from our house to Centennial Park, shot Louise, and rushed back to our house to undress and pretend to be asleep when Domenic Lawrence turned up on my doorstep.

"Did Miss Albright seem disturbed about anything last night?"

"No, she seemed just as usual—very pleasant and poised."

"Had she any enemies?"

"No, she was very popular. She had a number of friends —both men and women."

Finally, after all the questions and answers, which seemed only to prove that Louise had been shot by accident or by a maniac, I asked, "What about funeral arrangements? As far as I know, Louise had no relatives."

"We'll release her body tomorrow." He paused delicately. "If you want to make the arrangements—"

I said in relief, "Yes, I will. I think she'd like me to do it."

He picked up a report from his desk. "We wired Chicago. They haven't much on her. Apparently she'd lived there for a number of years with a widowed aunt."

I nodded. "She told me her parents died when she was very young, and she lived with her aunt and uncle in various places in the Midwest. Then her uncle died, and she and her aunt settled in Chicago. After high school, Louise held secretarial jobs for a time, and studied music part-time. Then her aunt died, too, and left some insurance, so Louise decided to use the money to continue studying piano full-time."

After I'd finished, I signed a neatly typed statement and went from the bright, garish lighting of police headquarters out into a downtown street so strangely normal, with people hurrying home from work, that it seemed unreal.

I stopped at Enright's Funeral Home and talked to a hush-voiced Mr. Enright before I went back to Greenwood Place. There I went straight upstairs and stretched out on the clean white counterpane. I lay there a long time, deliberately closing my mind to reality, allowing myself to think only of the lamplight on the gleaming old cherry wood of the dresser. Carefully I counted and recounted the nosegays of forget-me-nots in the wallpaper, until at last the flowers swam together and became a patch of blue water, and I slept.

If I had not been so tired, I might have been afraid, that first night alone in the little house, but I was in a state of numbness composed of fatigue and compounded by shock, which made me immune to outside circumstance.

Several times I heard the telephone's dim ring, and once I got up to go to the bathroom, and was horrified at the sight of my dead-white face in the mirror. Thomas came up from the kitchen and spent much of the night curled against the curve of my body. I left the lamp on all night.

Wednesday went by quickly. The police came and searched Louise's belongings, but it was plain enough, from their faces, that they'd found no clue to her death. I showed them her books and clothes politely enough, but some stubborn little nugget of secrecy made me conceal the existence of the secret room, which seemed peculiarly my own possession, bequeathed me, as it were, by Miss Grimes.

I was glad when they went away at last, and I could get ready to go to the funeral home. Barbaric though the custom is, I felt that someone should be there to greet the mourners, to receive the sympathy of the living for the dead.

So, in early evening, I walked the few blocks to the funeral parlor and was met by the undertaker, who pressed my hand with his own smooth, bloodless hands and murmured meaningless little bits of sympathy.

My first sight of Louise, a waxwork figure in her satin-lined coffin, shook me, but I moved away, and stood there, straight and unmoving, as the visitors came in, in little groups. They murmured their condolences, signed the guest book, and drifted away, uncomfortable, as people always are in the presence of death.

In her two years in Newton, Louise seemed to have met a great many people. For the most part they were musicians: graduate students and teachers from the conservatory, the music-and-art crowd who made a sort of club of the Ferris Wheel. Then there were a number of people from the city's social set. It seemed to me that Louise had had a very catholic taste in friends.

Those I did not know came and introduced themselves to me, and I looked at each of them carefully, wondering if one of them could be Louise's murderer.

Cecily Andrews drifted toward me, in her languid, boneless fashion. She was very small and dainty, and I had heard Louise tell her calmly that her beautiful duplex was a pigsty. Cecily, who had been married briefly at nineteen, had a small, beautiful daughter whom she boarded out during the week and took home on weekends. She was doing graduate work at the conservatory, and I assumed she was collecting a rather handsome alimony, since she lived in luxurious squalor.

"I'm so terribly sorry about Louise," she said in her customary careless drawl. Cecily always sounded as though the words she uttered had no real importance, either to herself or anyone else.

Then she asked casually, "Has Lucien been here?"

"He was here a little while ago," I said. "I think he may be out in the anteroom."

She sauntered off, looking quite impossibly chic among

the funeral flowers. Her clothes were always high-fashion, and her sleek brown hair done in the latest, most extreme style. She was carrying on a desultory affair with Lucien King, a handsome light-skinned Negro who was studying voice at the conservatory.

I shook hand after hand, feeling a little false, because I was not, after all, a grieving relative. It was sad that I, who had known her only a few months, was the only one to stand beside her coffin.

I scarcely recognized the ravaged face of Felix Reichmann, who had been with Louise briefly on Monday night, according to the newspapers, and who had been questioned by the police, then released.

"Sydney," he said, and his round boyish face was pale as death. "I can't believe it. Can you believe it, Sydney?"

He kept casting little, sidelong looks at the coffin and at Louise's face, waxen and doll-like on her satin pillow. I seriously thought he might faint.

"Come and sit down, Felix," I said, taking his hand.

He gave one more sickish look at Louise, then followed me to a chair in the corner.

Felix taught piano and arranging at Hoffman Conservatory. He was one of those good-looking, sweet-faced young men who never seem to change or grow older. He was well-read, charming, and popular. I'd been, with Louise, to a cocktail party at his apartment and had found it bright and cleverly decorated. Everything that Felix did, in fact, he did with a sort of flair. He was so eminently suitable as husband material that I'd been surprised Louise hadn't taken him more seriously.

"He's sweet," she'd agreed once when I'd suggested this to her. I remember she sat there fitting a cigarette into a silver and ivory holder, as though that were more important than the subject in hand. "But not for me, Sydney."

I'd wondered at her indifference, but of course I hadn't met Domenic Lawrence then. It was a case of exchanging a boy for a man, I suppose.

"I met her just as she was coming out of the library,"

Felix said, in the dazed tone of someone who has repeated his story so often that it has no meaning for him. "I was late for a meeting, but I offered to take her home. She said no, she liked walking in the rain, but I could take her as far as I was going, down Sutton Avenue. I dropped her near the entrance to the park, but I warned her she'd better take the long way around, instead of through the park. She just laughed at me. She said the park was right in the heart of the city, and well lighted, and she'd walked through it lots of times."

He dropped his head in his hands. "If I'd insisted on taking her home, she might be alive now. She would be alive now. But I just waved at her and went on to that damned alumni meeting."

I sat quietly, letting him talk, letting my gaze roam the crowded rooms. I was surprised to see, through the archway, Tony Ferris, owner of the Ferris Wheel, with two weasly little men who looked for all the world like mobsters. Louise had played piano for Tony, who didn't seem the type of employer who pays condolence calls; yet there was a huge basket of flowers from him, and there he undeniably was, in person.

There were Phil and Irene Valenti, too. Phil, who played the violin like an angel, was concert master of the Newton Symphony and taught at the conservatory. Irene, his wife, a spectacularly lovely redhead in her middle thirties, did nothing except adore Phil. They had no children, and she went everywhere with him, carrying his music case, making him comfortable, remembering for him, worrying for him. In his turn, Phil was almost paternally benevolent toward her. They came toward me now.

"This is a terrible thing, Sydney," Phil said warmly, pressing my hand between his warm, firm ones.

I liked Phil. Of all Louise's friends, he seemed to me most down-to-earth, most sincere, and the finest artist. And there was something touching about his dependence on Irene and hers on him. He was perhaps a little below medium stature, and stocky, with tightly curled black hair and anxious dark eyes.

Irene said little, but looked beautiful and remote, following Phil's face with her incredible eyes.

Over the heads of the others, I suddenly saw Domenic Lawrence. He went to the casket, stared silently at Louise, and walked away, speaking to no one.

When I was watching him, an exquisitely pretty young girl came up to us, followed by a young man as attractive, in his own way, as she was.

"I'm Paul Fleming," he said, his tone hushed, "and this is my fiancée, Barbara Carmichael. We're—I'm afraid we're the ones who found Miss Albright. We saw you at the park Monday night, Miss Webster, but perhaps you didn't notice."

I smiled at them. They were so clean and young, so obviously removed from death and fear.

"It was nice of you to come," I said. "That must have been a pretty terrible experience."

The girl nodded quickly, her eyes still drowned with remembered horror.

Paul Fleming was looking at Felix. "How are you, Professor Reichmann?"

Felix looked up dully and said, "Oh, hello, Fleming."

"Paul and I are both studying at Hoffman," Barbara Carmichael said, in response to my look. "I've seen you sitting in your office, Miss Webster, but I doubt if you've seen me."

I smiled apologetically. "There are so many students, and I've been there such a short time . . ."

They left then, and I went back to stand near Louise. Felix scarcely noticed when I left him. I longed to go home, but the two rooms were filled with people. I wondered if all of them had known Louise, or if some were curiosity seekers. The smell of funeral flowers, heavy and cloying, filled the air. The subdued lights, the muted voices, made the atmosphere dreamlike.

My head throbbed with pain, created by tension, compounded by the overheated room, the suffocating odor of flowers. I picked up my handbag from a chair near the casket and reached inside for the tin of aspirin I had put there earlier.

The tin was there, along with pen and compact and lipstick and the dozen other items every woman carries in her purse. But there was something else as well: a sheet of plain white typing paper, folded through the middle, and pasted on it, in words and letters cut from magazines, the chilling message: LEAVE TOWN, MRS. MACKENZIE, IF YOU WANT TO STAY ALIVE.

I went into the tiny ladies' room and swallowed two aspirin. I powdered my nose and combed my hair. Then I went back into the hot, crowded room, where so many people were shuffling over the silky Oriental rugs.

I talked, I listened, I smiled, but all the time I sought the face of the one who knew my well-kept secret, the one who wanted me to run.

# 4

*The hidden room.*
—CHESTERTON

After visiting hours, Phil and Irene drove me home from the funeral parlor, although they urged me kindly to stay with them.

"No, no, thanks. I'm not afraid to stay alone," I insisted. "I lived here alone for a time, before I decided to advertise for someone to share expenses. I'm used to it."

I went inside my little house, and for a long time I sat at the kitchen table, with the lights burning brightly, among the used coffee cups and the overflowing ashtrays left by the police. Then I jumped up suddenly and emptied the milk-brown coffee dregs into the sink, brushed cigarette stubs into a metal trash can, and tipped the basket of odorous coffee grounds into the garbage bag. Sergeant Tolucci and his men had been grateful for the hot beverage, and making and serving it had given me something to do, as I listened to the heavy feet pacing overhead in my little house.

I washed the cups and saucers in the hot suds and stacked them in the dish drainer. When I was finished, I wiped off the old wooden drainboard and surveyed the big old-fashioned kitchen carefully. I felt a sort of compulsion to keep Miss Grimes's domain as she had left it.

Something was teasing at my brain, and while I waited for it to manifest itself, I poached myself an egg and made toast and tea. As I sat down at one end of the scrubbed wooden table to consume my maiden-lady meal, I thought with a little pang of nostalgia of Louise, who had been something of a gourmet. Disregarding my modest food budget, she had come home often with the MG loaded down with

brown-paper bags full of exotic foods: anchovies and kip-
pers and a pot of Dijon mustard, and small, outrageously
expensive jars of truffles and caviar.

The fragment of memory became more tangible now. I
could see the MG, the day Louise had moved into 1 Greenwood Place. That day the sports car had been crammed to
the doors with her smart luggage, with a record player and
portable typewriter and books. In point of fact, she had
made a half-dozen trips from the apartment hotel where she
had been living in chilly comfort, and I had helped her
carry her things into the house.

On her final trip, the car had been less crowded, and I'd
picked up from the seat a handsome locked briefcase, made
of rich brown leather. Louise had taken it from my hand,
laughing a little.

"Looks businesslike, doesn't it?" she'd said, and had
taken it away to her room. That was the only time I'd ever
seen it.

The police had not taken away the briefcase when they
left, so it could not have been in her room. Too, I knew that
they had searched her car and found nothing of significance.
Nice young Sergeant Tolucci had told me that.

Quickly I got up and put my plate and cup in the sink and
went into the tiny foyer. I climbed the curving stairway with
its lovely, sweeping railing, and stopped on the landing. I
pressed the hidden catch beside the mirror, and the entire
panel slid to one side, revealing the small room. My hand
found the wall switch inside the room, and I went in.

The night-quiet of my little house was doubled, tripled
in here. It seemed lonely tonight, rather than merely safe,
but I shook off the feeling. It was best to make my search
when I was sure of being uninterrupted by the police.

The hidden room was very small, its floor covered with a
bit of green Brussels which might easily have been there
since Civil War days. There was a rather lovely piecrust
table and an ancient easy chair with sagging springs, and
an antique sofa whose upholstery needed replacing. Against
one wall was a glass-doored mahogany bookcase, jammed

full of dogeared copies of the Rover Boys, the Campfire Girls, and the Bobbsey Twins. There was no window, but the walls, papered with a faded rose-patterned wallpaper, lent a feeling of outdoors to the small room.

There was nothing else there, but I had put my metal strongbox, filled with clippings and personal papers, on one corner of the bookcase. It occurred to me that Louise might have left something of the sort here.

With beating heart and an inexplicably guilty feeling, I began to search the tiny room, inch by inch, and at last I found what I sought.

She had tucked the brown briefcase into the bottom of the old leather chair, up against the springs, and had refastened the burlap over the bottom with thumbtacks.

I pressed the lock with my thumb and gave an exclamation of frustration. The case was locked.

Uncaring now, I ran down to the kitchen and found a screwdriver in one of the drawers. Then I went back to the secret room and closed the panel again.

Recklessly I pried up the lock and opened the case. There was only one thing inside: a brown-paper parcel, tied neatly and carefully with strong white twine, knotted tightly at intervals.

The typed label read:

Miss Heather Smith
554 Fenton Street
Toronto, Ontario
Canada

There were no postage stamps affixed yet; otherwise the package was ready to go.

I hesitated only a moment. Then I thought: In for a penny, in for a pound. I slid the string off and opened the packet.

Inside was a small department-store cardboard box, and inside that, five hundred American dollars, in small bills.

# 5

*There is a strange charm in the thoughts of a good legacy.*
—CERVANTES

When I went out of the room and closed the door behind me, I heard the doorbell pealing peremptorily. I looked at my watch; it was ten-thirty. I ran down the steps and opened the door a little way.

The figure of Domenic Lawrence standing there, as he had on Monday night, was a shock to me. Go away, I wanted to say; go away, thou harbinger of death.

"May I come in?"

I opened the door silently.

He followed me into the sitting room and stood there, fingering a little pewter inkwell on the desk.

"I should have spoken to you at the funeral home," he said at last, "but I didn't feel like talking."

Then why have you come? I wondered. I waited in silence until he spoke again.

"I suppose you know," he said finally, "that Louise left you everything she owned."

I gasped, then laughed, and he looked at me sharply, out of those clever, unreadable dark eyes.

"I'm sorry," I said, "it sounded so important, somehow, when all she had to leave were her books and hi-fi set, and all those clothes, of course, but they'd be too small for me."

Then I thought of something else. "And her car, I suppose. But I couldn't possibly accept that."

I thought he was watching my face, to catch a change of expression, a flash of avarice, perhaps.

"Louise," he said, his voice carefully noncommittal, "left you her car, her personal possessions, and ten thousand dollars, part of an insurance policy from her aunt, plus wise investment, of course. Louise was a good business-woman."

I swallowed. His thoughts were plain as spoken words in the quiet room. Ten thousand dollars, for someone as obviously penniless as you are, my girl, is a great deal of money. That's worth killing for, isn't it?

Through a gray ribbon of cigarette smoke, Domenic Lawrence was studying me, his dark eyes unfathomable now.

"It's—it's ridiculous," I protested. "Louise must have had distant relatives, friends, *someone*."

"Apparently not." He was waiting.

My voice rose a little. "Well, I won't take it! It wouldn't be right. I didn't know Louise well enough to be considered a really close friend. She must have someone nearer to her." I looked him straight in the eye. "You, for instance, Mr. Lawrence. If you were planning on marrying her, why shouldn't she leave her money to you?"

He looked at the cigarette flame. "I said I'd thought of marrying her; that doesn't mean she had thought of marrying me. Perhaps she left it to you because she thought you needed it."

Privately I found it hard to believe that Louise *hadn't* considered marriage to Domenic Lawrence. He had a sort of tough charm which I should have thought would appeal to her. To most women, perhaps.

He took an envelope from his pocket and slid it across the gleaming surface of the desk.

"Read it," he commanded. "Louise left it for you."

I held it, studying the neat inscription, "Sydney Webster," reluctant to open the letter from those dead hands. But he was waiting, and I tore an end off the envelope and pulled out the single sheet of paper.

I skimmed the brief typewritten lines, and then the letter dropped from my nerveless fingers.

He picked it up and handed it to me.

"I don't mind admitting that I'm tempted to read this,"

he said. "Her letter seems to have made a fairly disastrous impression on you. I might say that this is the first time I've seen any obvious emotion on that face of yours." His dark look belied the compliment implicit in his next words. "You're as chastely beautiful, Miss Webster, as a Grace Kelly or an Audrey Hepburn, and just about as unapproachable."

Crumpling the paper between cold fingers, I said composedly, "It's a personal letter. Louise very kindly asked me to accept her bequest, because she knew I could use the money. She said she had no close relatives."

"Well, then," he said pleasantly. "It's all settled, isn't it?"

"Nothing's settled." My voice, to my dismay, was shaking. I got up and walked away, so that he wouldn't see my face. "Would you like a drink?" I asked at last.

Recklessly I splashed Louise's Drambuie into her crystal brandy snifters. I sat very straight on the green-velvet sofa, swirling the pale golden liqueur about in my glass, and wishing that I were on the Isle of Skye, which produces Drambuie. To me the very name sparkled with purity, creating in my imagination that little island, with its craggy peaks, its clear mountain streams rushing headlong to meet the sea.

The thought, invigorating as a dip in that sea, came to me then: with Louise's legacy I could take a trip to England and Scotland, shake off once and for all the memories which still clung to me. But the thought of Scotland brought me inevitably to the name Heather and the brown-paper parcel I'd found in the hidden room.

I drained my glass and set it down. "Would it be all right," I asked firmly, "if I were to take Louise's car for a day or two? There is something I must do."

He raised those sardonic eyebrows in polite inquiry. "Wouldn't it be wiser to ask permission of the police? They're the ones who might object to your leaving town."

"I mean to ask them," I replied coldly. "I only wanted to know how you feel, as her attorney, about my taking the car."

He got up, standing tall and forbidding in the fire's flickering light. "Since the car is to be yours, I see no good reason why you shouldn't use it. There will be formalities later, of course, but I'm sure no one is going to question your right to the automobile."

He picked up his topcoat from the chair where he'd dropped it.

"Thank you for the drink," he said politely. "And I apologize for intruding so late in the evening, but I thought you might like to have that letter. It was in a personal file in my apartment, and I could see no good reason for showing it to the police."

His eyes were hard and bright as flint. I hated him.

"That was kind of you," I said coolly, walking ahead of him to the door. "Good night, Mr. Lawrence."

"Good night, Miss Webster."

After he'd gone, I crouched on the hearth rug and reread Louise's letter:

Dear Sydney,

In the unlikely event that anything should happen to me while I'm single, I want you to have "everything of which I die possessed," as the books say. Thanks to a stockbroker friend, I've made some lucky investments with what was left of Aunt Minna's money.

Isn't it strange, Sydney? I've no one who's close to me. My parents are dead, and the aunt and uncle who reared me died several years ago. I'm a loner. Perhaps this is what draws me to you.

You see, I saw a newspaper photo of you, Sydney. Tony Ferris sometimes gets the Los Angeles papers; he used to live there. I recognized you. I'm sorry about your husband.

Use the money to buy the house, why don't you, if Miss Grimes will sell? I know you love the place. And have fun with the MG.

Probably you'll never see this letter. I suppose a mouse ran over my grave.

Best to you,

Louise

I folded the letter carefully and put it back in the envelope. I could think of only one thing: if Louise had known about me, someone else in Newton might have seen my picture too, and recognized me, even though there had been an interval of several weeks before I came east. It had been a poignant picture. Someone had seen me, the person who had put the note in my handbag, the one who knew I was Sydney Webster Mackenzie.

I got up stiffly, aware of the chill of autumn seeping into the little house, which had seemed to me so safe and quiet a haven. I went up to the little room and locked Louise's letter in my strongbox. Then I copied the name and address on the package into my address book.

I had already made up my mind that I would go and find Heather Smith, to whom Louise had been about to mail several hundred dollars. I'd call Captain Morley first thing in the morning, to tell him that I had to go out of town for a day or two. I didn't think I'd mention Toronto.

## 6

*There's rosemary, that's for remembrance . . .*
— SHAKESPEARE

The engine of the little MG sang like a bird as I wheeled
her along the throughway. Overhead the deceptive skies of
October shone blue as lapis lazuli, with white-cotton clouds
drifting lazily here and there. I was seized by that illusory
sense of freedom which a journey always brings. One has
the feeling that all problems are left behind, all bills paid,
that any painful letters will never catch up with one, and
therefore do not exist. One will keep driving endlessly,
peacefully, watching the fields swim past, hearing only the
rush of the wind and the swift passage of other automobiles.

I went across the bridge at Niagara Falls, scarcely glancing at the beautiful waters rushing below. I had seen the falls
once, during my thirteenth summer, when we'd come east
to spend the long, hot, languid months in Poughkeepsie,
with my grandmother, who lay dying in a breeze-filled upper
room. Mother and I—I remembered it clearly—had gone
on a two-day trip to Niagara Falls, leaving Dad alone with
his frail little mother.

At Customs, I declared mine a "pleasure trip" and said
that I would be back in the United States in two or three
days' time.

Then straight down the Queen's Highway we sped, the
MG and I, past the neat battalions of brick houses which
make Toronto and its environs so different from the American cities across the border. I became filled with impatience
at the long line of traffic which converged on the city, for
I felt quite strongly that some of the answer to Louise's death

lay in this quiet city, whose very atmosphere proclaims its Scottish and English ancestry.

A few miles from the city, I found a pleasant motel called the Queen's Inn, left my luggage in cottage Number 5, and drove on into Toronto to seek a late luncheon.

I left my car in a parking lot and walked along Yonge Street, stopping in a tremendous, brightly lighted bookstore to buy two mystery novels and a street guide.

After that I found a basement tearoom and went down the stone steps into a nearly empty restaurant. A smiling waitress led me to a table.

"The mixed grill is good today," she suggested.

"I'll have that, then," I said, handing back the menu. "And I think a dry martini, please." I had need of extra courage today.

While I sipped the cocktail and looked about the dark-paneled dining room, dim even in midafternoon, I pretended to myself that I was Sydney Webster, traveler, here on the first leg of a leisurely journey, unknown and unknowing.

Still with this pleasant, unrealistic feeling, I consumed the grilled chops slowly, savoring every mouthful, and finished off with a pot of very hot tea. While I enjoyed the tea, thinned down to perfection with water from the second pot, which never seems to be served in American restaurants, I took from my bag the guide to Toronto's streets. I was here for a purpose; it was no good pretending otherwise.

Fenton Street branched off one of the streets which crossed Yonge, and I had already ascertained that Yonge was one of the main arteries. Reluctantly I paid my bill and ascended the stone steps to the bright sunshine outside.

Walking slowly, gazing in shop windows, I marveled at the unhurried atmosphere of the city. Cars traveled in a leisurely fashion along the narrow, winding streets, and drivers waited courteously for me to cross the intersections.

Wondering by now what I had imagined I could accomplish by this improbable trip, I got my car out of the parking lot and drove down Yonge for a mile or so. After a few twists and turns, I found, without much difficulty, 554 Fenton Street.

It was a shabby brick apartment house, the sort of place I knew by heart; Jed and I had lived in enough of them. They are the same in San Francisco as in Toronto. All over the North American continent, I suppose, these semirespectable, drab edifices stand, grim refuge for the poor, the old, the unattached. I mounted the high stone steps and pressed the bell, wondering what I should say, now that I was here.

The woman who came to the door was painfully thin, with gray hair still streaked with blond. She wore two pathetically misplaced spots of rouge on her thin cheeks.

"Does Heather Smith live here?" I asked boldly.

She looked surprised. "Well, she did. But she moved out of town over a year ago. She had a chance to go to Scotland and England, and she took it."

I could have cried with disappointment. The one miserable little clue, for which I'd had such high hopes, had led straight up a blind alley.

The woman hesitated, seemed on the verge of saying something, then closed her thin orange-red lips.

But I was emboldened to ask, "Did she leave a forwarding address? I'm terribly anxious to get in touch with her."

She hesitated again, and then apparently the urge to talk to someone, to take a few moments away from the dull routine of her everyday existence, got the better of her.

"Why don't you come in?" she said. "I have a post-office-box number for her somewhere. She still gets letters occasionally. She asked me if I'd hold her mail for a friend to pick up, because she wasn't sure what her address would be, traveling around Europe, and all."

I followed her into a hallway I knew like the palm of my hand: dark, clean enough, but fusty-smelling and dismal, with mud-brown linoleum on the floor. Poor Heather, I thought, no wonder you snatched at a chance to get away from this.

Monica Kelly—she'd told me her name before I was

fairly inside the door—led me into a living room only slightly less gloomy than the hall. The enormously high ceilings made the room as unhomelike as possible, even though the front window was banked with bright geraniums and begonias and a flourishing aspidistra.

It was unnecessary for me to answer her vague questions; she was so thirsty for talk that she went on and on, without stopping, and all the time her hands were busy, picking up faded newspaper clippings and bits of notepaper and limp snapshots.

"Did you say Heather was a friend of yours? I don't remember meeting you. But then, she was a very reserved girl, never brought many visitors here. Pretty as a picture she was, though, with that soft dark hair and those gay little ways. Dainty, you know, and neat as a pin. My mother thought the world of her. She wasn't a bit surprised when Heather got the chance to go to Europe as secretary-companion to some rich woman. Mama always said Heather would make her mark in the world."

My heart sank as she rattled on and on. The Heather emerging from this welter of words was hardly sinister: a pretty, dainty, efficient girl working her way up in the world. I wasn't sure what I had hoped for, but it certainly was not this.

"My mother died last year," Miss Kelly said, "and left the apartment house to me. Of course I'd managed it with her, ever since I left high school, anyway. . . ."

I'd stopped listening, because the picture she was painting of her life sounded so hopeless, so drab and friendless. Sydney, you pig, I said scornfully to myself. What have you been moping about, all these months? So you had a terrible experience. So what? You're only twenty-five years old, and you've health and an interesting job.

And Domenic Lawrence, my traitor mind continued, said you were as chastely beautiful as a Princess Grace or an Audrey Hepburn.

I pulled my mind away from the thought of Domenic, so dark, so knife-keen, so ready to think me liar and murderess.

"Oh, here it is," Monica Kelly said at last, extricating a small blue leatherette memorandum book from the conglomeration of papers and booklets. "I found this notebook in Heather's room after she left. It had slipped down in the side of a chair. So I hung onto it. You can look through it, but I don't think she has any forwarding address in it."

I could see a few lines written on the page she held open, and my fingers itched to get at the book.

A clanging set up suddenly in the rear of the house, and she said distractedly, "That's the grocer's boy. I don't have a car, and it's cheaper for me to buy where they deliver. He'll want his money, though."

I got up hastily. "I must be going anyway. Thank you so much, Miss Kelly. I'll let myself out."

I followed her into the hall, and she went, with her quick, nervous gait, toward the kitchen.

Feeling like a thief, I ran back into the living room and hands trembling with eagerness, snatched up the little notebook and thrust it into my coat pocket. Then I let myself quietly out the front door.

## 7

*A little street half garden and half house.*
—TENNYSON

I drove away from Fenton Street quickly. My heart still thudded painfully in my ears, and I hoped guiltily that Miss Kelly wouldn't miss the little notebook.

After that I drove around the streets of Toronto, past the Royal Ontario Museum and the Parliament buildings, around the university, then to look at the battlements and the gray towers of Casa Loma.

I had had a late lunch, so I drove back to the motel after my sightseeing tour, to watch television for a while and to study the neat back-handed script in the little memo book and wonder about the people whose names were written there.

Finally I lay on the narrow bed in the gathering dark, thinking of the unknown girl, Heather Smith, whose life must somehow have touched that of Louise Albright. The name, Heather, so lovely, so virginal, reminded me of the garden at 1 Greenwood Place, where heather grew in sweet, wild clumps.

Behind Miss Grimes's house there was a long, narrow patch of backyard, enclosed on three sides by a high wall, its time-pinkened brick dressed discreetly in a garment of heavy green ivy. Tiny rambler roses, half-opened, poked their shy, crimson faces over the wall, and bluebells tinkled a soundless tune. The peonies, ruby-red and gaudy in their beauty, subdued the muted orange of the tiny Indian paintbrushes.

I had sat there, in my first weeks in the little house, watching the branches sway in the summer breeze, listening to the music the wind made as it sighed through the leaves and tickled the thin blades of grass. Occasionally an airplane would soar far overhead, and the city's traffic, so short a distance away, roared dimly. I had then—and liked—the feeling that I was alone in a small world of my own.

In August, I decided, reluctantly, that it would be wiser to share the expense of the house, and Louise answered my advertisement and moved into the place. She and I soon became friends in that oddly reserved, oddly easy way of two persons who demand nothing of each other. I did not pry into her personal life or her antecedents, and she maintained a similar restraint with me. We were as polite and dainty as two cats who have been thrown by chance into the same household, and decide to accept each other's presence graciously, if not warmly.

But I was the Cat Who Walked by Himself, and Louise was not. She was scarcely settled in, her suitcases and books and cartons unpacked, when she asked if I would object to a party.

"Of course not," I said in surprise. "Why should I mind?"

She lit a cigarette and sank down on her bed, among the little piles of silken sweaters and expensive lingerie.

"I don't know," she said casually. "It's just a way you have about you. I imagine you might think parties a waste of time."

Not a waste of time, I thought, just something over and done with, something put away with my lost youth. There'd been no parties in the series of cheap, furnished one-room apartments to which Jed and I had fled; and just at first, when things were better, we'd been too much in love to want other people. I turned my thoughts away from Jed, with his boyish face, his ingenuous, innocent smile.

Louise stubbed out the half-smoked cigarette in a tiny golden purse ashtray which must have cost considerably more than my handbag itself.

"You're new in town," she said. "You should meet some people."

"You're very kind." I could scarcely tell her that I still

wanted to run from people like a frightened animal.

"I'm not kind at all," she said calmly. "You'll find that out soon enough. But I can talk to you, Sydney, and when I think of it, I realize there's no one else in the world to whom I really can talk."

She got up and went to the window and looked out at the walled garden, where late roses still flung their sweetness wantonly on the thinning air.

"Sydney," she said, and it seemed to me that her voice came from a great distance, "doesn't life sometimes seem completely useless, completely empty? All the things I've done, good or bad, I've done because they seemed like a challenge at first, and then when I've conquered them, and the challenge is gone, they're worse than useless, and I ask myself why I bothered."

I didn't trust myself to answer.

But it got better after that, and there were days when I forgot my unhappiness and talked giddy nonsense, as though I were as gay and carefree as Louise and her friends. I attended Louise's first party, and her second and third, and met the sweet-and-sour mixture of types which formed her little coterie, and I tried to lose myself in the contemplation of other lives.

I took out a cigarette now, and lit it, inhaling the first pungent whiff of tobacco. Then I thought: What a silly habit this is; and I crushed the orange glow into an ashtray decorated with a picture of the motel.

I got to my feet then, went and washed, and put on a dress, so that I could go out and have dinner and perhaps see a movie. Tomorrow I would check over the few clues in Heather Smith's little memorandum book.

When I went out, shivering in the October wind, the tree-lined court was silent and dark, its nether corners dimly lit by carriage lanterns. Only a bit of night wind riffled the green glossiness of the ivy leaves clinging to the walls of the cottages. A cat, silvery gray in the light from one of the windows, stalked regally across the tiled patio, and I thought, with a sudden passionate homesickness, of Thomas, shut brooding in the cellar, with his dishes of food and water and milk.

Feeling a little lonely in a strange city, where no one knew me or cared who I was, I drove back into Toronto, found a likely-looking restaurant, and had my solitary dinner. After that I saw an uninspiring foreign film.

When I emerged from the theater, the bright lights gave me a disjointed feeling, as though I were cut off from everything safe and familiar. I went into a little coffee shop and had a final cup of black coffee, and this helped to dispel the disembodied feeling.

After that, I bought Canadian magazines in a drugstore, got into the car, and drove back to the motor lodge.

There were a number of cars parked in the drive, but the motel was not full. The place was quiet, and most of the lights were out, even though it was only midnight.

I got out of the car and locked it carefully. Then I started toward my own cottage. Suddenly, a car came roaring up the long sweep of driveway which gave onto the court.

The headlights, which had been turned off, were switched on full, blinding me. As the car hurtled at me, straight up the paving stones of the little courtyard, I jumped, and as I did so, I realized, in sheer amazement, that I wanted to live.

I thought fleetingly of Jed, and then the right-front fender caught me and flung me onto the patch of lawn in front of one of the cabins. Before I could get my breath, the automobile, colorless in the night, suddenly reversed and aimed itself at me, as a projectile at a target.

Gasping, I tried to scream, and suddenly, blessedly, lights came on in a cottage, and a man and woman ran out onto the minute porch. The car went tearing down the court toward the highway.

"Oh, what is it? What's happened?" the woman was saying, over and over again.

She and her husband came and helped me to my feet. She was middle-aged, her gray hair in rollers, and she wore an aging bathrobe. Her kind face was filled with distress.

The man, a stocky, balding person, tried to calm both of us.

"Are you all right, young lady? Are you hurt? Emma, she'll be all right; calm down."

The woman, still chirping in dismay, led me into the cabin, where she began to brush at my clothes ineffectually, but in the kindest possible way.

"I really am all right," I insisted.

The man said, "We were sure we heard a car coming up the courtyard!"

"Yes. It threw me onto the grass."

I found that I couldn't possibly tell them the real truth: that someone had aimed his auto at me deliberately, as deliberately as one aims any deadly weapon.

These good, unimaginative people would have thought it fantastic; but even if they believed me, they'd want to call the police, and my mind shrank away from any more official questioning.

"Crazy young drivers," the man said severely. "They probably had one drink too many and were showing off."

I let it go at that, and they led me back to my own cottage and saw me established safely inside. When they had gone, I snapped the night lock quickly and put the chain across the door, and still I stood there, trembling, trying to shut out evil.

The door was cool against my bruised cheek, and I stood there for a long time, letting it ease the pain. Once I had stood like this beside Jed, while a policeman had waited outside. Then Jed had gone, out the window, down the fire escape, and at last I'd opened the door to the officer. I'd answered his polite questions, regally at first, then brokenly, as the import of those questions reached me. And that was the first moment, the moment when I'd seen Jed for what he really was. . . .

I went into the bathroom, turned on the bright light over the washbowl, and sponged my rapidly swelling cheek with cool water. The face which looked back at me was pale with shock, except for the purpling bruise, and the eyes were smudged in, their green made brighter by the weary shadows under them. But the face was no longer remote. It was alive with something more positive than fear, something more urgent than unhappiness. Anger.

I was consumed by a blazing fury toward this person who had attempted brazenly and openly to run me down, as though I were some creature which must be destroyed, by whatever means possible. The threatening note I had found at the mortuary had been no practical joke. Someone wanted me dead, as Louise was dead. Someone had gone to the trouble of following me all the way to Toronto, had tried to run over me.

The anger felt good, refreshing as a dip in an icy mountain stream. I'm alive again! I thought.

My hands still shaking, I took the little travel kit from my suitcase, filled the cup with water, and heated it scalding hot with the immersion heater. I put in a tea bag and watched in satisfaction as the amber color darkened the water. Then I swallowed two aspirin, to ease the pain in my cheek and head. Wrapping my feet in the blue blanket which had been folded neatly at the foot of the bed, I sat sipping my hot tea, planning what I should do on the following day.

Gradually the warmth of the hot liquid spread through my body, and I relaxed against the pillows, ready for sleep. Before the blanket of sleep covered my brain completely, I had decided to go back into the city once more, in the morning, and see if I could track down more information about Heather. It seemed self-evident that someone didn't want me to find out about her, and this made me stubbornly determined.

Still, I fell asleep with the lights blazing.

## 8

*Perseverance is more prevailing than violence.*
—PLUTARCH

In the morning the MG and I threaded our way through the traffic into Toronto, in limpid air, crisp and sunny and invigorating. In spite of myself, I was beginning to feel a little thrill at the chase, a mystery reader's excitement at the untangling of a skein of events.

I found a parking space and went into a Lyons tea shop to have breakfast. How lovely and normal the people looked! The waitresses, crisply clean and friendly, the businessmen with their morning coffee and their folded newspapers, the smart young office girls having a quick breakfast before trotting off to work on their impossible heels.

While I ate the toasted English muffin and drank the inevitable pot of tea, I studied the little memo book which had belonged to Heather Smith. Out of the mists which surrounded this girl, these were the only realities, these half-dozen names and addresses, jotted carelessly among the bits of memoranda in the little blue book.

"Lipstick, stockings, toothpaste," ran one list, and then just beneath it, in a neat backhand, "Joe Burnham, 19 Sailer Place, LU 6-4320."

On another page, after a list of recordings, the name "Mary Harrington, DU 3-1345" was scribbled. Well, at least, I mused, Heather Smith was left-handed; her clear, definite script showed that. But it was little enough to go on. I wondered what percentage of Toronto's population was left-handed.

I decided to try Mary Harrington first, but I dawdled a bit over my breakfast, enjoying the lull in the sunny busyness of the little shop. Then I went to the telephone and dialed the number.

"Tracy's Coffee House," said the brisk young voice.

"May I speak to Mary Harrington, please?" I said authoritatively.

"This is Mary Harrington." There was a questioning little lilt to the voice.

"Do you happen to know a girl named Heather Smith?" I asked. "I'm trying to locate her." Then I added hastily, "This is an old friend of hers from the States."

"Oh, I haven't seen Heather for at least a year," the girl said. "I'm awfully sorry. She used to come in here for dinner at night, and we became quite friendly. We went out on double dates once or twice, as a matter of fact. But she had a marvelous offer to go to Europe, and she left the city in a hurry, quite some time ago."

My heart sank. I said slowly, but without hope, "Do you have her address now, by any chance?"

The voice said cheerfully, "No 'fraid not. I did have one postcard from her, from New York City. She was to sail the next day, and that's the last I heard from her. Of course, I really didn't expect to hear. I hadn't known her very long, and I suppose she must be pretty busy, working and sightseeing."

I thanked her and hung up slowly. My trip had come to seem silly and unnecessary. What had I hoped to accomplish by tracking down this innocuous young woman who'd gone off to Europe on her own very proper and sensible business?

I went back and ordered coffee this time, and sat drinking it, rich and dark and hot, until its own peculiar qualities brought order and clarity back to my brain. After all, Louise *had* addressed a package to Heather Smith, and she had enclosed in that package a considerable sum of money. Would she have done this for a girl known to be in Europe?

There was no answer to these questions, but I was determined to find out something, discover some thread which tied Heather Smith of Toronto, Canada, to Louise Albright of Newton, New York.

Number 19 Sailer Place was easy enough to find, a dingy antique shop, up a curving cobbled street, in an old and rundown section of the city. The bow windows were filled with blue Wedgwood, lovely as a piece of spring sky in their drab setting.

A sweet tinkling bell announced my entry to the young man sprawled reading in a delicate Windsor chair. He wore a rough gray sweater with leather patches on the elbows, and shaggy light-brown hair fell across his forehead. There was a severe beauty about his face, bent over a volume of T. S. Eliot.

Looking up, he said idly, "May I help you, or would you like to browse around?"

"I'm not shopping," I said. "I'm looking for Heather Smith. Do you know her?"

His look on me was wary and suspicious, the look of a man somehow at odds with the world.

"Sure. I know Heather. Why?"

The question was out there, bold as brass, and fairly unanswerable. Why did I want to find Heather Smith? Because I felt that she might have been blackmailing Louise? Because I felt she might be implicated somehow in Louise's death?

Yes, to both, although common sense told me that Heather could have had little to do with Louise's actual murder, if she really was in Europe. But there was a tie-in somewhere, and this ungracious young lout might be the answer.

"Look," I said, as boldly as though I had the right to ask questions, "it's imperative that I get in touch with Heather Smith."

"Well, you can't." There was triumph in his gaze. "She's in Europe. She took a job there last year . . . more than a year ago."

I changed my tactics, let my voice soften, as I said, "I'm really terribly anxious to get in touch with her. Don't you have a forwarding address?"

His cool blue eyes measured me, and I rather thought

they found me wanting. He didn't really believe that I was Heather's friend.

"I don't think I'd like to give any information to a stranger," he said.

Dropping all subterfuge, I said frankly, "My name is Sydney Webster. I've come all the way from Newton, New York, and I must find someone who knows Heather Smith. Are you certain she hasn't returned from Europe?"

There was a little conscious swagger to his shoulders as he said, "I'm sure she would let me know if she decided to come back."

Pulling a battered cigarette pack from his pocket, he extricated a cigarette, without offering me one, and lit it. Drawing on it deeply, until the lighted end was a small fire, he said casually, "Just why would you come here looking for Heather?"

I told him then about Louise's murder, about finding the packet of money addressed to Heather. It was a relief to tell someone the whole thing, to share my dangerous piece of information.

When I'd finished, he sat staring at me for a while, his face flushed a dull red.

"You must be crazy," he said at last, flatly. "Heather was as poor as a church mouse when she lived here. She never had two coins to rub together. As soon as she got her salary and paid her rent, she rushed out and bought something to wear, or something beautiful but utterly useless. I was always giving her hell, she was such a spendthrift. But as for money, real money, that's absurd!" He added incredulously, "I get your meaning, don't I? You think Heather was blackmailing your friend Louise?"

I said stubbornly, "Unless they were close friends, and Louise had some other reason to send her all that cash, yes, that's what I mean. It must have been blackmail. People usually send checks through the mail, you know."

His look was scornful. "What good would it do Heather to blackmail your friend, all the way from Europe? How would she collect the money?"

If she *is* in Europe, I thought silently. She needn't have told you when she returned.

He grew a bit more expansive. "She worked here, you know. I met her here. This is my uncle's shop, and I worked my way through the university by helping nights and Saturdays. Heather was his full-time clerk for about a year."

Somehow he made me see her, small and dainty in her blue smock, her face, under its dark hair, pretty and beguiling. She had loved the Wedgwood, the pewter pitchers, the pieces of copper and brass, the old ivory-and-lace fans, the wooden butter churns, the spinning wheel. She had handled the old china dolls gently and dusted the ornate candle sconces and the gilt-edged mirrors.

The portrait he painted of Heather was more seductive, less lonely and friendless than Miss Kelly's view of her, but it was still an innocent picture, nothing like my idea of a hard-bitten blackmailer.

"Do you have a snapshot of her?" I asked suddenly.

"No," he said, and there was a chill in his tone once again; he'd remembered that he was talking to an enemy.

Deflated, I began to wander about the shop, wending my way between barrels of ancient books with musty bindings, among tables and shelves heaped high with a careless display of worthless trifles arranged indiscriminately with some rather lovely pieces of china and Bristol glassware. There was even an old wooden carrousel horse, its brown paint scratched and pitted, its big eyes mournful. My hands lingered on its flank, but I knew it would be a ridiculous piece of extravagance.

A green-glass paperweight caught my eye, and I took it to the sales counter recklessly, not even bothering to ask the cost. Joe Burnham got to his feet slowly and put the paperweight into a small box for me. I noted that he handled it gently, wrapping it in tissue.

"There," he said insolently, handing me my change. "It matches your eyes, you know. Green glass." The implication was unmistakable. Yet I could remember when my eyes, my face, had been vulnerable with love and tenderness.

"Glass breaks," I said quietly. "Someone tried to smash me last night, Mr. Burnham. I'd like to find that person before he tries a second time."

A startled look flicked across the imperturbable face. "What do you mean?"

I told him then about the car which had raced up the courtyard of the Queen's Inn and tried to run me down.

When I'd finished, he said reluctantly, "It sounds serious enough, but I fail to see any connection with Heather. Why are you so determined to find her?"

"I've told you: that parcel of money addressed to her. Your Heather is tangled up in this somehow."

I thought he looked rather pleased at that; he liked having her called "his" Heather. I wondered why he'd let her go away, if that was how he felt about her.

"Look, Miss Webster," he said finally, after a rather heavy silence, "quite honestly, I haven't heard from Heather since she left for Europe well over a year ago. But I do know that she went occasionally to visit some ancient relative of hers, on one of the islands across from Toronto. The only trouble is, I don't know the address."

I fished the little blue memo book out of my purse and riffled the pages excitedly. "Would this be it?" I asked. "Mrs. Sarah Hungerford, Maple Street, Moon Island?"

His closed-in face opened with surprise for a moment. "Where did you get that?" he demanded, and I thought he was about to grab the book from me.

"That's unimportant," I said. "But thank you for your help, Mr. Burnham."

I went out of the old shop quickly, feeling his hard gaze on my back.

# 9

*Is there anybody there? said the Traveller,*
*Knocking on the moonlit door.*

—DE LA MARE

The squat old ferryboat, with the water lapping at its sides, and the gulls swooping down around it, bustled with activity. I mounted the gangplank in a sort of dream, conjured up by the waves and the cool sunlight's dance on the clear waters.

The captain, in a shabby, comfortable uniform, was jolly as a boat captain in a film. The passengers, pleasant and relaxed, as people are when going on a boat trip, however short, climbed the stairs to sit in the sunshine, but I took a seat on the lower deck, near the railing.

I watched the Toronto skyline slide away and become a muted pinkish gray. Then I turned my attention to the boat, as it cut its neat swath into the shimmering lake water, the furrows of green falling away from the prow. It was pleasant, being mesmerized by the emerald glow of the water, and I gave myself up to it for a time.

But presently I saw the lush and verdant island, and I began to wonder about Mrs. Hungerford, for hers was the only remaining address of any importance. The others were only those of a dry cleaner, a hairdresser, and a record shop.

When the boat pulled in to the dock, I asked directions of one of the passengers, then set off to find Mrs. Hungerford's house. The island was not large, and inside ten minutes' time I had found the street I sought.

Set well back on its deep-green lawn, the monstrous white house was an architectural nightmare, with its mansard roof, its many cupolas, its captain's walk. Some profligate hand had flung onto the rambling frame structure every disconnected bit of decoration available in the early 1900's.

After several minutes Mrs. Hungerford answered the old-fashioned bell pull. She was a slight gray feather of a woman, with wisps of white hair hanging about her face.

"Well, come in, come in!" she said impatiently in a small, thin voice when I'd told her I wanted to talk about Heather Smith.

I followed her into the dim entry hall and thence to a sitting room. The house's desolation shocked me. No sunlight could have penetrated these rooms for many years; ivy grew thickly over the windows, and cracked green shades were drawn to the floor on the two long windows facing the street. The smell of dust, of age, of disuse permeated the air.

Mrs. Hungerford perched in temporary fashion on the edge of a sagging horsehair sofa.

"Well," she said fretfully. "What did you want to tell me about Heather?"

"I understand she used to visit here," I said carefully. "I'm very anxious to get in touch with her."

She wrapped her skinny arms about herself, the bird-claw hands clutching protectively at her thin shoulders.

"You're up to something, young woman! What do you want of Heather?"

"I just want to talk to her."

"Well, you can't." Her false teeth clicked together firmly. "She's away. She's in Europe."

Heather Smith. Address: Europe. Still, I pursued the subject hopelessly.

"Surely someone must have her address there. Doesn't she write to you?"

"She sends me money to live on." Her face tightened suspiciously. "Are you here looking for my money?"

I said hastily, "No, no. Of course not." I hesitated, wondering if I should reveal the depths of my ignorance about Heather. "Is she a relative of yours?"

She looked at me as though I'd taken leave of my senses. "I'm her granny! I thought you knew that."

Heather's grandmother! That ephemeral creature, float-

ing through a world of mists, had roots after all; had a
grandmother and a home, albeit that home was like something out of Edgar Allan Poe.

"If she sends you money, then surely you must have her
address," I persisted.

"She's traveling around," the old woman said vaguely.
"She left her belongings in the cellar and she went off. She
told me to write to American Express in Paris and London
and places. But I never write letters."

I could believe this. The beginnings of senility were
written plainly on her wrinkled face and in the faded, uncaring blue of her eyes. Arteriosclerosis had made its inevitable inroads on that old frame and that fogged and
cloudy mind. People would mean little to her these days;
the figures of her youth would be more vivid to her by
tomorrow than I myself would be.

I wondered if she used Heather's money to buy food and
fuel, or if it was tucked in useless little packets about the
drafty old house, to be found after she was dead.

I rose to go, and thought of one obvious question. "Do
you have a picture of Heather, Mrs. Hungerford?"

Looking more like a feather than ever, she drifted about
the room, stirring up the dust on the long-closed piano and
on the heavy mahogany library table, as she picked up and
put down the faded brown portraits which cluttered those
pieces of furniture.

Finally she chose a framed photograph and handed it to
me. "That's Heather," she said proudly, as though it pleased
her to recognize her granddaughter.

With beating heart, I took the picture from her and looked
at it.

I could have laughed aloud. The portrait was of a little
girl on a pony, a small, pretty child, perhaps nine years old,
with dark curls tumbling onto her shoulders. There was an
imperious tilt to the lifted chin, and her mouth was unsmiling. She sat the piebald pony as though he were a handsome
mount of her own, instead of the wretched decoy of some
itinerant photographer.

Character traits I might deduce from that delicate face, those unsmiling, self-contained lips; but I would not recognize Heather Smith if she were to sit beside me on the ferry returning to Toronto.

"She's lovely," I said gently, setting the picture on top of the piano.

Mrs. Hungerford rearranged it carefully on its own special island of dust.

"Pretty as could be, that child was," she said in satisfaction.

"Well, thank you very much." I edged toward the door, and she followed me, wafting along behind me as though blown by a strong wind.

The shadows were lengthening when I stepped out onto the grass-grown walk. I heard the night lock snap into place behind me, and then the house slipped back into its oblivion.

Past the tourist homes and summer cottages I hurried, past the little tea shops, the gift shops, past the small restaurants with their inevitable "Fish and Chips" signs.

A needlelike autumn rain had begun, and I buttoned my coat against it. I had nearly an hour to go before the ferry would return to the mainland, and I decided to stop and have an early dinner. I turned in at a small, green-painted building with the screen door still hanging there from summer.

It was like bursting into sunshine, after a day of storm and gloom, to enter the little restaurant, with its small round tables and shabby, comfortable booths. The lamps were cozy little pools of yellow, and the smell of fish, crisp and freshly fried, hung pleasantly in the air. I savored the hominess of it, after the musty chill of Mrs. Hungerford's ancient house.

After the simple, home-cooked meal, served on thick white china, after two cups of excellent black coffee, I leaned back against the cool leatherette of the booth and lit a cigarette. Mesmerized, I watched the thin thread of smoke and let my brain go blank. It was a method which often worked for me, when I had a problem to solve: the releasing of the matter to my subconscious.

It had been there all the time, of course, lurking in the back of my mind: if I could get back into old Mrs. Hungerford's house, perhaps I could look through Heather's belongings in the cellar. It was foolhardy, perhaps even dangerous, but it was the only solution I could see.

"Would you care for more coffee, miss?" The round-cheeked, white-aproned woman who had waited on me smiled at my absentmindedness, awaiting my answer.

I ordered another cup of coffee and sat sipping it while I planned my strategy. Would she let me in again, that vague, forgetful old woman, or would she be too fearful, too fiercely protective of her home and her treasures?

I got up swiftly, paid my check and left. There was still a faint drizzle in the air, and the night had become cool. There were almost no people on the quiet, tree-lined streets, and the island seemed preternaturally silent after the bustle of Toronto. Away off in the distance, I could hear the faint music of a rock-'n'-roll group, playing for some teen-age dance, and voices sifted through the partly open windows of some of the tourists' lodgings; but no one was foolhardy enough, on this wet fall evening, to sit on a front porch and notice the passing of a female stranger in a dark raincoat and a kerchief.

Silent as a thief, which indeed I was, to all intents and purposes—I knew that now—I found my way without difficulty to Mrs. Hungerford's Victorian house. It was in total darkness. Either she had gone early to bed, or else she sat, like a silent specter, watching the rain make little puddles in the muted glow of the streetlamp. By no stretch of the imagination could I picture her out drinking tea with the neighbors or watching television in the privacy of her bedroom.

No dog barked as I approached the house, and I could feel that she slept, as the aged sleep, somewhere on the second floor of the old house. Her thin, veined hands would be fluttering even in slumber, and her soft old mouth, the false teeth removed, would be sunken as though in death.

Boldly, in complete silence, I went up the flagstone walk

and then, unchallenged, I picked my way toward the back
of the big house. The smell of rain-wet zinnias was heady in
the night air, and I knew that I could connect them forever
after with this night. I was consumed by fear and guilt, yet
I had come too far not to make this one last effort to solve
the mystery of Heather Smith.

There was an old cellar door, of the style built on an
angle, divided in the middle, with each half lifting up
separately. This one was ancient and weatherbeaten, and
the rain was pouring through one broken corner.

I pulled on the rusted metal handle, and the heavy door
came up. By the light of the tiny flashlight on my key case,
I found my way down the worn, uneven steps. There was no
inner door to block my way, and I entered a vast, cavernous
cellar. It was pitch dark, except for the tiny stream of weak
light from my flashlight, and for a moment my heart failed
me. Then I saw a single light bulb suspended on an electric
cord, above two stationary tubs. I switched on the bulb.

I went up the smooth, damp stone steps and pulled the
heavy door in place, to keep out the fine rain. Then, back
inside, I went up the wooden steps which led to the first
floor and found, as I had expected, that the door was securely locked from the kitchen side. In the unlikely event
that the old lady should come into the basement at this time
of night, I would hear her fumbling at the lock and could be
outside before she had the door open. I had already decided,
should anyone see and question the cellar light in this secluded house, to brazen it out by saying that I was a friend
of Heather, sent to collect her belongings. It seemed highly
unlikely, however. The street had been quiet and deserted,
and seemed likely to remain so.

The cobwebs festooning the heavy old beams, the broken-
down look of the old upright washing machine, the general
look of disuse, told me that no one ventured into the cellar
these days, and I breathed a little more easily.

The trunk was a fairly new brassbound footlocker, the
sort sold in department stores for college students and camp-
ers, and I was certain that it was Heather's. It was locked.

On a long wooden table I found a rusted hammer and chisel, and I went to work recklessly on the snap lock of the trunk. It gave quite quickly, and I pulled up the hasp. My heart was thumping like a gong inside my chest.

There were no personal items in the locker, no trinkets, no photographs or pressed corsages, no old clothes. Instead, there were three bankbooks, each on a different Toronto bank, each made out in the name of Heather Smith, at her grandmother's address, and each recording very sizable amounts of money. There was a bulging ten-by-thirteen manila envelope.

I looked over the bankbooks, totaling the amount roughly at upwards of fifteen thousand dollars. A young woman who has fifteen thousand in cash is not likely to accept a position as companion to some demanding old lady, even if the reward is a trip to Europe. Heather Smith, judging by these bankbooks, could quite easily have financed her own trip.

I looked at the dates on the bankbooks. The last deposit had been made four months before, yet Heather was supposed to have been in Europe for the past year. Someone— Joe Burnham, for instance—could have made the deposits in her name, of course, but I had believed him when he said he hadn't heard from Heather Smith for the past year.

I opened the big brown envelope, and instantly I knew whence Heather had derived her rather large income. It was jammed with clippings and photographs, old letters and type-written résumés on a variety of people, all residents of Newton, I thought. I saw the names of people I knew: Cecily, Felix Reichmann, Phil and Irene Valenti, Tony Ferris. I would read them later, but a cursory glance had told me that all the facts gathered in this file were unpleasant ones, loose bits of information which, tied together, formed a pattern for blackmail.

I closed the trunk carefully and pushed the lock down so that it would look undisturbed. Then I turned off the dangling bulb and went up the stone steps into the slanting rain.

The house was still dark and silent, and I pushed my way

past the wet, overhanging branches along the side of the house, toward the front. I wanted the place to be dark, wanted Mrs. Hungerford to be safely asleep, yet at the same time, I longed for a light, a sign of life, something to comfort me.

I made my way to the street without incident, and clutching the lethal envelope to my side, underneath my raincoat, went back in the direction of the little restaurant where I had eaten dinner. There was no one about, and this gave me an eerie feeling. The summer resort was closed in, half-deserted, a ghost island for ghost people like poor old Mrs. Hungerford, with her cracked green windowshades and her vague, peering ways.

I had missed the last ferry, of course, and it was frightening to realize that I had nowhere to stay on this night when the walks were black with rain. I walked aimlessly for a bit, then, pondering the credibility of my story, I mounted the old-fashioned veranda of one of the lighted tourist homes and rang the bell.

There was a suffocatingly long wait, then the bright porch light came on, and a plump, graying, middle-aged woman opened the door and peered out at me.

"I know it's off season," I said diffidently, "but I've missed the ferry, and I wondered if you might have a room?"

She hesitated, looking me over carefully in the bright yellow light of the porch bulb, while I, conscious of the incriminating brown envelope under my arm, waited tensely.

"We don't have many guests at this time of year," she said at last, "but there's a room ready, and an adjoining bath, if you want it."

"Yes, yes, I'd like that." I was conscious of overwhelming fatigue, brought on, I knew, by the tension created by breaking and entering.

"My luggage is in a motel in Toronto," I explained, as I followed her into a comfortable hallway, up thickly carpeted stairs to a second-floor bedroom.

Mrs. Tait gave me towels and soap and asked if I'd care for a cup of tea or coffee.

"I would like a cup of tea," I said gratefully. "The rain is so cold now."

Politely she refrained from asking what on earth I'd found to do in the rain on Moon Island on a dark October night, and certainly I was not about to explain myself. We smiled at each other, and she went down to make the tea.

"I'll bring it up when it's ready," she said.

"No, no, please. Just give a shout and I'll come down for it."

I was glad she hadn't suggested that I drink it downstairs with her and her husband, who had been watching television in the living room as we'd passed. I wanted rather badly to get a closer look at the contents of that envelope.

I took off my wet raincoat and hung it on the closet door to dry, then looked about gratefully. The room was comfortable and homey, with three white-painted walls and one papered cheerfully in red Colonial-patterned wallpaper. The big double bed was white-painted iron, old-fashioned and comfortable, and there was a little radio on the bedside table.

I heard Mrs. Tait's voice calling, "Miss Webster, your tea's ready." I wondered if I should have given her a false name. It was unlikely that the envelope would be missed in the near future; still, it might have been smarter to have made no obvious connection with the island.

I went to the stairway and took the tray she proffered. "It looks wonderful," I said. There was a brown earthenware pot of tea, a jug of hot water, milk and sugar and a little plate covered with a napkin. This, I discovered when I was back in my bedroom, was a blue plate of homemade fried cakes such as I hadn't tasted since my mother's death. Propped on the bed, my shoes and dress off, I ate the doughnuts and drank the bracing tea and looked through the contents of the envelope.

There was a dossier on Cecily, and its contents scarcely surprised me: pictures of Cecily and Lucien, snapped while they were sitting close together in Cecily's car, and photographed, entwined together, on a sandy beach. I wondered who had photographed them, and how. A telescopic lens, perhaps? At any rate, someone had cared enough to follow them, to photograph them, to save the evidence, someone who knew that Cecily stood to lose her little girl if her behavior was anything less than circumspect.

Felix Reichmann: a card-carrying member of the Communist party in his college days in New York City—days when rebellious college students, instead of staging sit-ins, had become Socialists or Communists, as a form of protest against the Establishment.

Pictures of the back door of the Ferris Wheel, and a famous member of the Mafia entering arm in arm with Tony Ferris, were there. The two somber faces were turned to each other, the nearest thing they knew to a smile evident on each dark face.

What careful, painstaking brain or group of brains had prepared these dossiers, had gathered up bits and pieces of information, with a photograph here, a newspaper clipping there, a Xeroxed line from a city directory, a personal letter, all of which, taken together, formed a damning whole?

Sydney Webster: There was a newspaper photo, a very clear and perfect picture of me, being lifted from the pavement, being torn away from Jed's body. My long, fair hair blew in the wind; my face was a perfect mask of grief, and the caption read: "Mrs. Sydney MacKenzie is removed from the body of her slain husband, Jed MacKenzie, holdup man who was shot while escaping from the police."

The name was MacKenzie, but the face was quite evidently that of Sydney Webster. I saw all my heartbreak there in one very clear tabloid picture: a human-interest picture, they called it.

The appalling thing about the collection of misery in this bulging envelope was the fact that someone had tracked it all down, minutely, painstakingly, mixing, sifting the tiny facts, putting them together to form an unsavory whole. There was nothing of good here; each bit of information was damaging.

Feeling unclean, I took my fluffy blue towel and washcloth and the bar of soap and went into the big, old-fashioned bathroom to wash. Then, scrubbed and refreshed, I went back to my cozy room and propped myself against the pillows to read further.

The material concerned only people from Newton, mainly people I did not know, prominent citizens I'd read about in the society columns. All their little foibles and follies were here, laid bare for the reader. Most of them, I knew, would be immensely threatened by the revelation of the bits of information, even in this day of liberal morals.

The preponderance of material about Newton made me fairly certain of one thing: Heather Smith was not in Europe. She was in Newton. It all fitted together: Heather the blackmailer, with her bulging envelopes of notes about the people of Newton, had to be a resident of the city. Some of the items were of recent vintage; one or two clippings were dated less than six months before, which meant that she had not been in Europe at the time, as Joe Burnham and Monica Kelly believed her to be.

It seemed perfectly plain to me that Heather was living in Newton, doubtless under an assumed name, and that, either singly or in collaboration with others, she had carefully and systematically uncovered damaging evidence against a number of people, with a view to blackmailing them.

I wondered if all of them had paid: Mrs. Norbert Van Orden, for instance, leaning intimately across a lamplit table, smiling fondly into the eyes of someone even I, a newcomer to Newton, knew was not her husband. Mr. Van Orden's picture was often in the papers. He was much older than this blond woman, a respected, honored doer of good civic works. It would be easy, I reflected, to persuade Mrs. Van Orden to pay fifty or seventy-five dollars a month, say, out of a generous allowance, to keep her husband from seeing this revealing picture.

Finally I put the envelope aside and turned off the light and opened my window to the rainy night. It was very quiet here on the little island. There was the faint click of rain against the leaves, the whisper of the wind in the branches of the trees outside my window, and that was all. I was in limbo tonight, and the temptation was great to forget Heather Smith and her ugly bits and pieces of misery. With the money Louise had left me, I could go away from Newton, take that trip to the Outer Hebrides, perhaps, and restore my soul.

But lying there against the soft down pillows, listening to the gentle flick of the raindrops against the darkened pane, I knew that I wouldn't leave Newton just yet. I had to find Heather Smith and warn her to let her victims go. Once I found her, surely I could make her believe that I would tell the police if she continued her blackmailing activities. I knew that I wouldn't actually betray her victims to the police, but how was she to know that? And I had less to lose than the others. After all, my guilt was only by association; I had done nothing wrong except to marry Jed. I would be shamed and degraded if anyone in Newton were to know that my husband had committed robbery and been shot trying to escape, but I could endure it. I had endured worse; I had endured the loss of Jed himself.

Just before I fell into a wonderful, dreamless sleep, I remembered the car which had tried to run me down at the motel. Did Heather Smith already know of my existence, and realize that I posed a threat to her?

## 10

*The villain still pursued her.*
—MILTON NOBLES

Straight down the Queen's Highway I sped, letting the motor out easily. The air was bright October wine, that tangiest, most potent of distillations. For no very apparent reason, I felt something approaching happiness, or, more correctly, anticipation. It was so long since I'd felt anticipatory about anything, that it was like a totally new emotion.

The Canadian maples flamed red and gold and bronze against the azure backdrop of the sky, and I felt ready for anything. Anger and indignation, whirling and churning in my body, had wakened me at last from the long sleep which unhappiness had produced.

At that moment I would have given my eyeteeth to have seen the car which had tried to kill me at the Queen's Inn. In my mind's eye, I saw only a tremendous dark shape hurling itself at me like some giant bird of prey. At any rate, if the same car was following me now, I could not distinguish it.

With a little triumphant squaring of the shoulders, I determined that I'd give him a run for his money, whoever he was, if he should be traveling with me. I set the MG at a steady pace and sped along, the wind licking at my hair, the sun patting my cheek.

At the Peace Bridge I looked sharply at every New York State car I could see, but there was no one I recognized. And indeed, I realized, as I set off down the throughway, I hadn't really expected to recognize anyone. The person who was after me was no open assailant. He—or she?—came treacherously in the night, a lone and secret enemy, using darkness as a shield. He would not show his face, this adversary, because I would recognize it.

My heart began to thud tumultuously. Here was truth. The person who had tried to kill me must be someone I knew, someone I'd recognize. That meant someone from Newton, one of Louise's acquaintances, probably, since my own social contacts had been limited.

All the way home, a journey so uneventful as to lull me into a fleeting sense of security, I thought of this new idea: the person who wanted to kill me was someone who knew both Louise and myself. Strangely, I never gave a second thought to the idea that my intruder had anything to do with Jed. His dark and hideous story had burst like a bombshell upon the clear and gentle innocence of my life and of my love for him; but now he was gone, and there was no reason to think Jed could affect me in any way.

But there'd been murder done, and I couldn't get over the feeling that someone who visited the little house at 1 Greenwood Place had done that murder. Racking my brain, going over every bit of information I possessed about Louise, I still couldn't find anything which pointed to her slayer. Yet there must be something there, and I must possess—or, at any rate, the murderer believed I possessed—a bit of incriminatory information, a piece of information important enough to make him commit murder again. I felt a thrill of pure terror, then, as I realized that my death would have looked like an accident, and who would have cared?

My parents had died, as faithful in death as in life, within weeks of each other, and there was no one else who mattered particularly, certainly no one who knew where I was living now. Old friends, an aunt and uncle and cousins, would have read with sadness and nostalgia of my death, would have said, "So young, too. I see that she took back her maiden name after her husband died. Sad, sad thing. Sydney was such a pretty girl, and so bright. Her mother and father had such hopes for her."

The police? Captain Morley couldn't be expected to take any special interest in one murder witness who took herself off to Toronto and got herself killed by a reckless teen-ager. And thank God, I thought, shuddering, the Newton police apparently had found no reason to get in touch with the California authorities about me. At any rate, no one had identified Sydney Webster of Newton, New York with Mrs. Sydney Mackenzie of San Francisco, Sacramento and Los Angeles.

The return trip was without incident, and I might have believed that I had read something sinister into the incident at the motel, had it not been for the angry red gravel burns on my left forearm, and the bruised cheekbone. These were real enough, and every time my arm touched the car's armrest, it reminded me that someone must find the murderer before he should find me.

## 11

*Treat your friend as if he might become an enemy.*
—PUBILIUS SYRUS

With one great, glad cry of recognition, Thomas came bounding up the cellar steps. He leaped onto the kitchen counter and began to rub his hard, furry jaw against my face as I bent over him.

"Oh, you're a handsome one, Thomas," I said, opening the package of ground beef I'd bought and putting a large portion in his dish.

He ate it quickly, and looked up at me hopefully.

I shook my head at him. "The other half's for *my* supper," I said.

The bell whirred, and I said, "Damn," and went to answer it. It was Cecily.

"Where've you been?" she demanded, as though she had a right to know. "I've been calling and calling."

I said shortly, "I had to go out of town on business. Was it important?"

Somehow she was inside, and before I knew it, I was mixing her a martini while she draped her small, boneless body on the sofa.

"Aren't you having one?" she asked languidly, sticking out her hand for the sweat-beaded glass.

"It's too early in the day for me," I said impatiently. I often found myself wanting to hit Cecily; she was so lazy and so imperious. "What's on your mind?"

She sipped the pale, cold liquid for a few minutes before she said, in a tone quite different from her usual disinterested drawl, "Sydney, you know my little girl, don't you?"

"She's a darling," I told her sincerely.

Cecily's voice was flat. "I'd put my hand in the fire for her any day."

I found myself liking her better than I had done at any time in our brief acquaintance.

"I'm sure you would, Cecily," I said gently.

She turned her eyes away from me and dropped those extravagant lashes against the pain.

"My ex-husband is getting married again, and he wants Tina. If he had even the tiniest inkling about Lucien, he'd have me branded an unfit mother and have her taken away from me. He has the money to do it; his family is one of the richest in Detroit."

I filled her glass again silently, then I took the bull by the horns. "Cecily, forgive me for asking something you'd consider none of my business—but are you being blackmailed?"

The sleek head jerked up, the amber eyes became cold as glass. "Why should you ask that?"

"I have a valid reason. Wait a minute."

I went into the kitchen, where I'd left my luggage. Somehow I had hoped Cecily would bring up the subject of blackmail herself, but I could see now that the reason for her visit was either loneliness or boredom, or both.

I unlocked my suitcase and took out the photograph of Cecily and Lucien. When I went back to the living room and handed it to Cecily, her cool little face showed no emotion whatever, and I had a moment in which to wonder if I was making a vast mistake, if all my calculations and suppositions were wrong.

"I rather thought this was material for extortion," I offered.

She looked at it briefly, distastefully. "Are you trying to blackmail me, Sydney?"

The rush of fury was almost pleasant. It meant that I could feel again, could experience anger and indignation, after all the months of deadness.

"At least give me credit for some intelligence," I said coldly. "If I were your blackmailer, would I be likely to tip my hand?"

She shrugged, and I added, "And thanks for your good opinion of me. It's nice to know that you think of me as a potential blackmailer!"

Cecily smiled her cool little smile. "I don't suppose I did think that, actually. But how did you get hold of that photograph, which my darling ex-husband and his parents would love to lay hands on?"

I countered with another question. "Do you know anyone named Heather Smith?"

She shook her head, and I felt that she was telling the truth, although Cecily commonly lied with all the ease and facility of a cat sliding gracefully through a spot seemingly too small for its body. "Should I?"

I said carefully, "I think, whoever she is, she's your blackmailer."

She narrowed the beautifully made-up eyes. "That's your assumption, not mine. I've said nothing about blackmail."

I sat down wearily in Miss Grimes's big wing chair and kicked off my own shoes. "Oh, come off it, Cecily. I'm not going to tell your ex-husband, or anyone else. Please tell me the truth. Maybe we can figure out Heather's identity, since I'm certain she doesn't use that name. I've checked the telephone book. She must be someone you've met."

She looked at me for a moment. "What can I lose? Sure, someone is blackmailing me—not for a fortune, just for a neat, tidy little monthly sum, which I take out of my alimony." She added grimly, "There'd be no alimony if Ross ever got wind of this."

I told her a little then, of my trip to Toronto, my foray into Mrs. Hungerford's cellar, and the fat pack of incriminating material with which I'd come back.

She looked completely astonished, which I considered a small feat on my part, since Cecily never showed any emotion stronger than disdain or boredom. "Breaking and entering! I'd never have suspected it of you, Miss Prim-and-Proper."

"I know. I can hardly believe it of myself. But I had to do something positive. Someone wants to get rid of me for some reason, and someone is blackmailing you and"—I gestured at the manila envelope—"and all these other people, I have no doubt. I can't take that bunch of filth to the police; it would be a betrayal of all these people. So I thought I might solve things by unearthing Heather Smith and warning her that I have her material, so she might as well cease and desist."

She looked at me oddly. "Don't you think it might be a bit dangerous, taking on a blackmailer?"

"It had occurred to me." Suddenly I felt friendly toward Cecily, expansive, as I'd never been with anyone in Newton, except, very occasionally, Louise. "What about another martini, Cecily? I'll have one with you."

I went into the kitchen and made the martinis, and some cold beef sandwiches to go with the drinks. I had a notion that Cecily didn't hold her drinks too well, and I'd had no lunch.

When I went back to the sitting room, I found her squatting on the floor, cross-legged, like a yogi, pawing daintily through the extraneous material in the brown envelope.

"Cecily!" I said sharply. "I didn't intend you to look at the rest of that material."

Her upward gaze was completely bland. "Oh, sorry about that. Misery loves company, you know. I wanted to see who else our friend Heather had trapped."

I gave her the martini and urged sandwiches on her. Thomas went and sat beside her mutely, his yellow eyes fixed on her face, until she surrendered and offered him scraps of roast beef. We ate and drank in a fine spirit of comradeship. Perhaps it was only the martinis, but Cecily seemed unusually friendly and down-to-earth today, the little veneer of cool sophistication replaced by an unsuspected warmth.

"I'm not exactly from the other side of the tracks," she said presently, "but I certainly wasn't brought up in wealthy surroundings, as Ross was. His family never liked me, and I never liked them." She took another pull on the cocktail glass. "Actually, I don't think Ross ever liked me much, either. He liked my looks, and it rather pleased him that I had talent, but he never approved of my friends or my family or my way of life. He likes life to be perfectly ordered, perfectly predictable. He wants Tina to be brought up that way. He wants *her,* and he and his parents would be perfectly delighted to have proof that I'm not a good mother. They're so refined, I doubt if they would stoop to having a detective watch me. But I'm sure they wouldn't be too proud to buy that photograph if it were offered them."

"Then," I said slowly, "it seems reasonable to suppose that Heather—whoever she is—knows that you are divorced and that you could lose the custody of your child if Ross were able to discredit you."

There was a long silence, while Cecily puffed on a cigarette. "But who?" she said finally. "If it's not you—and I believe that it's not, I assure you—who could it be?"

I went on to tell her of the envelope of money I'd found in Louise's briefcase, the money which had made me aware that Louise was being blackmailed, and of my journey to Toronto.

When I'd finished, she looked at me curiously. "Didn't it occur to you to tell the police all this?"

"Well, yes it did," I admitted. "But until I went to Toronto, I had nothing to go on. And now that I've found this material, I can't betray all these people to the police. That would mean they'd all be suspect."

She gave me an empty look. "Including me."

"Including you." I added quickly, "I won't give the police this material unless some part of it becomes vital evidence against Louise's murderer—if they ever find him."

I could have shaken her for her bland expression. "Please think, Cecily. It stands to reason that Heather Smith must be someone who knows you, knows your circumstances. Someone at the conservatory, perhaps?"

She was shaking her head. "Heather's a fairly uncommon name in this country. I'm sure I'd have heard it."

"Well, then, she's changed her name," I said impatiently. "Who knows about you and Lucien?"

She shrugged. "Dozens of people, I suppose. We're seen

together often enough, at school and at the Ferris Wheel."

She looked at me defiantly. "We try to be discreet about his visits to my apartment, but I suppose enough people suspect that, too."

I shook my head. "You really aren't bright, Cecily. If everyone knows about Lucien and you, what's to prevent Ross from finding out?"

"He's in Detroit," she said simply, "and I'm here. And I told you—he's too honorable to stoop to having me followed. Besides, we're divorced now. He'd have no reason. But he does want Tina rather badly. If someone offered him proof, he'd take it without a qualm."

Outside, the wind had begun to rise, and in the afternoon stillness, it sounded lonely and desolate. Cecily put her hands to her ears.

"I can't bear this quiet!" she said, with a sort of controlled frenzy. "Turn on some music, will you?"

I went over to Louise's hi-fi and switched it on. A Chopin prelude, one of her favorites, filled the room, and I thought, with a little pang of remembrance, that she would not hear its soft, unmistakable melody again, not in this life, at least.

Trying to shake off the loneliness, the sudden sense of futility, I lighted the gas log and turned to Cecily determinedly. "Tell me about the blackmail letters. When did they start, and how much have you paid?"

She leaned forward and stretched out small, bloodless hands to the blue fire. Her hair, smooth and glistening, caught the fire's light. Her voice was as low and as full of meaning as I'd ever heard it.

"It was ten months ago that the first letter came. It was addressed to me, by typewriter. There was a sheet of cheap typing paper inside, and it had words cut from magazine pages. It said, 'Would you like your husband to take away that pretty little girl? If not, send two hundred dollars to John Hutchinson, General Delivery.'"

She added bitterly, "I've been sending it every month since then, each time I get one of those notes. I daren't *not* send it." She opened her purse and took out a white envelope. "The latest one arrived today."

I took the letter from the plain, cheap envelope and looked at the uneven strips of printing, words clipped from magazines, strewn upon the page, like a child's first-grade work. "Your husband is anxious to have your little girl, isn't he? Prevent this. Send two hundred, Box 618, Buffalo."

The white envelope was dated the day before, postmarked Newton. It could have come from anywhere in the city.

"The police?" I suggested helplessly.

She shook her head. "I couldn't possibly," she said definitely. "Even if they found out who it is, it would be too late for me. He—she—would have told Ross by then. I know it. The money is of no importance compared to my child."

This, then, was the way a blackmailer succeeded in his dark and ugly pursuit: he counted on the guilty fears of his victims to protect him. The additional safety of this particular extortionist, of course, lay in his anonymity. A few scraps of paper, a box number, and no other tangible clue.

"Would it do any good," I asked Cecily helplessly, "to watch the boxes at the post office, or the general-delivery window?"

Slumping down onto the sofa, she lit another cigarette before she answered. "How could we?" Her voice held the familiar note of bored disinterest, as though she had explored all these possibilities and found them wanting. "He's changed his name and box number two or three times, and once I had to send it to general delivery in Syracuse under the name Henry Bartlett."

The cigarette ashes drooped like gray gauze onto the front of her dress. "The post office won't give out any information unless the police are involved—and I can't tell the police. So there we are. Full circle."

We sat on in the amorphous twilight, smoking, sipping our drinks, letting the moments slip off the day, like beads off a string, neither of us wanting or caring to hold them back.

Finally she got up, said, "Thanks for the drinks," and drifted off, as dainty, as unruffled as ever.

I went and sat at the kitchen table, under a bright light, and let Thomas rub his head against my face comfortingly. As I was thinking, idly amused, that Miss Grimes would undoubtedly faint at the sight of a germ-laden cat sitting on her shiny-clean table, the telephone's ring split the silence. I went into the sitting room to answer it.

The voice was silken-smooth, beautifully modulated, and quite indistinguishable as to owner.

"Sydney," it said gently, "I'm not finished with you, my dear. You are a meddler, you know, an interfering little busybody."

"Who is this?" I asked sharply.

The voice laughed a little. "A friend. Now, isn't that the proper answer? A friend."

I said angrily, "You coward! What is it you want of me?"

There was steel in the voice now. "I want you to mind your own business, Sydney. Otherwise your employer and your new friends are going to know all about your charming husband and his—occupation."

The line went dead, while I sat shivering in the half-dark. After a long time I got up, stiff and old, and put on the lights in the living room.

Why did the room seem changed tonight, seem inimical to me? The pretty, faded wallpaper, the deep-silled windows, each with its own windowseat, the faint, intangible odor of potpourri from the blue-sprigged bowl on the mantel, had always seemed to me like bits of a world long gone but faintly remembered. But tonight, even with the lamps lighted, even with the velvet draperies drawn against the chill dusk, the room was somehow hostile, and the china pug grinned evilly at me from his place on the whatnot stand.

I could think of nothing, the rest of that evening, but the telephone call I'd just received. The voice, smooth and unctuous though it was, had been sufficiently disguised so that I was uncertain of the sex of its owner. Was my enemy man or woman?

# 12

*All truths are half-truths.*
—WHITEHEAD

The Ferris Wheel was not half-filled yet; it was too early. I slid into a small booth, and Bill, the waiter, came up to me.

"A glass of sherry," I told him.

When he brought the golden wine, I gulped it down, and sat with my fingers wrapped tightly around the stem of the glass. I knew now why unhappy people drank; the wine, sliding down smooth and fiery, warmed temporarily the cold, lost, lonely pit of my stomach.

Another girl was sitting at the piano which Louise had played with such negligent skill. This one, a tall girl with long black hair and a perfect, disdainful face, accompanied her own sultry singing.

The dark little tavern was coming alive now, the customers wandering in, sitting on stools at the semicircle of the bar. The little lights winked and blinked and were caught up and reflected in the green and brown of the bottles on the shelves behind the bar. Fred, the bartender, touched bottle to glass, measured, served, smiled.

Tony Ferris waddled up to me and smiled, too close to my face. He looked like Khrushchev.

"What are you doing here, all by yourself?" he asked cozily, leaning over the table.

I forced myself to be cozy in return. "Just getting information, Tony," I said lightly.

"Information about what?"

I smiled at him, a painfully seductive smile, and he slid into the booth opposite me, as I'd known he would.

"Buy you a drink," he suggested. He glanced at my glass. "A real drink," he amended.

"Just a cup of coffee, thanks."

He shrugged and snapped his fingers at Bill, the waiter. When he'd ordered coffee for me and cognac for himself, he leaned across the table, breathing wine and garlic into my face.

"Now, what's all this about information? What do you want to know that I can tell you?"

I reached into my big leather bag and brought out a brown envelope with the clear, glossy photograph of Nick and the well-known Mafia man. I couldn't think exactly how to frame my question.

"Does this mean anything to you?" I asked lamely.

He looked at me, and I knew that I was afraid of him. "Where did you get that?" Underneath the faintly guttural English was the menace of a thousand years of brigands and cutthroats, of men lurking in dark Sicilian alleys, waiting for the poor, hard-working peasant making his innocent way home. I felt that, had we been in some lonely cul-de-sac, my life would have been snuffed out as quickly as he'd snapped his fingers at the waiter.

Bill brought the coffee and the cognac, and I was able to wrest my gaze from Tony's swarthy, heavy-lipped face. I kept my eyes on my cup as long as I could.

Then, "Where did you get that?" he asked softly.

"It doesn't matter. The point is—I think several people in Newton are being blackmailed. I think *you* are being blackmailed, Mr. Ferris."

His face went a sort of mottled gray. "Are you trying to shake me down, young lady?"

I looked at him boldly. "I wouldn't be so foolish. But I'm pretty sure Louise was being blackmailed, and I think she found out who the blackmailer was. I think that's why she was killed. I know she had been paying off someone, but she hadn't mailed the last payment, when she was killed."

He got to his feet in one supple, swift movement, amazing in so heavy a man. "I don't know what you're talking about.

I don't know nothing about blackmail. And if you know what's good for you, you'll give me that." He motioned a stubby hand at the photograph. "Then you'll forget you ever saw it."

I hesitated. I didn't want him to think I was intimidated, but I was. And I had no right to the incriminating picture, after all. Silently I handed it to him.

"That's better," he said, and got to his feet. "Bill," he said, motioning once again at the waiter. "Another drink for the lady." To me he said, without any expression at all, "See you around."

I shivered a little, remembering the time Louise had come into the house on Greenwood Place, early one morning, white-lipped and livid with fury. I'd been out to a rare concert myself, and had stood, in my elegant blue-silk cocktail dress, drinking tea before the fireplace.

"What's wrong?" I'd asked in amazement. I'd never seen real anger on her face before.

"If Ferris doesn't keep his fat little hands to himself," she'd said coldly, "he can find a new piano player."

Then she was gone, that cold and angry person, slipping away like a gray cat into the mist; and only the pretty, vivacious Louise, in her soft white gown, was left. I'd forgotten the scene until this moment, but now I wondered if that other Louise might not have shown her claws to Tony Ferris himself. For after all, each of us is at least two persons, one the person the world knows; the other, the hidden, secret, violent person who crouches like a tiger, waiting to spring out when our guard is down. If that sleeping tiger had lunged at Tony Ferris, might he not have killed in retaliation? I thought he might. I pondered the possibility that Tony Ferris might have had Louise killed because she had scorned him. And there, I thought, would go your fine theory that she was murdered because she refused to pay her extortionist again.

I found that I was really afraid of Tony Ferris. He was not a subtle man. His anger was swift and direct and vengeful. I could see my body at the bottom of a well, or sprawled on a country road, the victim of some hit-and-run accident, presumably. No, I dared not question further this man who could snap his fingers and dispose of me.

But why would a man like Ferris pay blackmail money? Wouldn't he have put some of his men on the case, found and eradicated the extortionist?

The man who walked in the door the next moment was so tall and broad of shoulder as to be immediately notice-able in that small place, inhabited by small, unhealthy men. It was Domenic Lawrence.

He saw me at once and came and sat down. "May I?" he asked belatedly, and I nodded.

"Well, what are you doing here, Miss Webster?" he asked. His tone, his look, said: Waiting for a pickup, waiting for someone to buy you a drink?

"And what are you doing here, if it comes to that?" I flashed back.

He looked around vaguely, frowning a little. "I don't quite know myself," he admitted, rubbing his fingers wearily along the bone of his nose. "It seemed like a good idea, when I left home, to come down here where she worked, and meet the people she knew best."

I found myself pitying him again. I looked around at the people, many of whom I'd met, on visits with Louise and her friends. The Ferris Wheel was the sort of small, intimate place, not especially elegant, but not shoddy, which has a little cluster of habitués as its center. They were nearly all here tonight: Claudia, the stout, attractive woman in her fifties, a quiet alcoholic, leaning her elbows on the bar, touching her bursting red lips genteelly to the glass of whiskey in her hand; Big Jack, three hundred and fifty pounds of flesh and drink, who came when the Wheel opened in the morning and stayed until its close; Lucien, with skin like coffee and cream, stroking the drums idly with the brushes, commencing the sensuous rhythm, the slow, languorous beat of the newest love song, following the dark-haired singer.

The handsome young couple entering the bar looked familiar to me. The girl, in a smart beige knit suit, with brown accessories and one dramatic gold pin on her lapel, was exquisitely pretty. When she chanced to turn my way, she smiled uncertainly and said something to her escort.

They came toward our table then, and I saw that it was Barbara Carmichael and her fiancé, Paul Fleming, the pair who had found Louise in the park.

"Hello, Miss Webster," Paul Fleming said, smiling.

How perfectly he matched his lovely companion. He was only a little taller than she, and he was handsome in that clean-cut, boyish fashion which is so peculiarly American. His suit was exactly right, casual, but of excellent cut.

"Good evening," I said. "I don't know if you've met Mr. Lawrence?"

"At the funeral home, I believe," he said respectfully.

Domenic Lawrence invited them to sit down and have a drink, and they did so, with that peculiar mature grace which seems a part of the fortunate young generation.

Sitting there quietly, I contributed little, letting their chatter run over me, like shallow water over stones. Something about these two hurt me. The girl, with her innocent, assured prettiness, was like myself, a thousand years ago; while the young man was so different from Jed that I almost hated him.

He looked at me gravely now, out of gray, sympathetic eyes. "Has there been any news about Miss Albright's death?"

"No news at all," I said, shaking my head hopelessly.

"The D.A.," Domenic Lawrence said suddenly, savagely, "is going to write this thing off as an accident. I can see the handwriting on the wall. No evidence, no enemies—no murder."

"Well," Barbara Carmichael said timidly, "it could have been an accident, couldn't it? Teen-agers fooling around with a gun, shooting it for fun, and hitting someone? They'd be afraid to tell, I should think."

Paul Fleming nodded. "That's the way I see it, too. Obviously Miss Albright was not the kind of girl who gets killed."

"Everyone is the kind of person who gets killed," Domenic said darkly. "Each of us has an enemy, somewhere, someone who hates us enough to do murder, if he could do it without being caught."

He paused, beckoned the waiter, and ordered drinks as smoothly as though he had nothing on his mind but providing a pleasant evening for friends.

Lucien was singing now, a calypso song, gay and light-hearted, yet somehow eternally sad. Even while my fingers moved involuntarily in time to the captivating rhythm, my mind was saying coldly: Everyone is the kind of person who gets killed. Sitting there quietly, letting my unseeing gaze rove politely over their faces, I remembered Louise's letter to me: "I suppose a mouse ran over my grave."

A mouse was running over mine now; the same mouse, I had no doubt. I shivered involuntarily, and when I looked up, they were all staring at me: Barbara Carmichael sympathetically; Paul Fleming, inquiringly; and Domenic Lawrence, coldly, it seemed to me.

I lifted my glass and drank, but when I set it down, I had to use both hands, to conceal the trembling.

I said defiantly, "I'm sure she was murdered."

Domenic Lawrence downed another Scotch; he was drinking quite a lot, I thought, but showing it not at all, unless in the degree of somberness.

"What makes you so sure?" he asked at last.

I shrugged and said nothing. How could I tell them that my own life had been threatened, that someone had attempted to run me down? They'd think me a silly, hysterical woman, anxious to share the limelight centered upon her dead friend.

"Oh, there're my sister and brother-in-law," Barbara Carmichael said, and I thought there was relief in her voice. "We're meeting them."

They left then, gracefully, as though the atmosphere had

become uncomfortable, and they were too well bred to linger.

"Now," said Domenic Lawrence adamantly, "suppose you tell me exactly what's going on. Why are you so sure Louise was murdered?"

To my intense annoyance, my voice faltered, though my tone was haughty. "I don't know that it's anything to do with you!"

He gave me a dispassionate look. "I think it has a great deal to do with me, since it concerns Louise."

It was a shot in the dark, but I aimed it boldly. "Did you ever hear of Heather Smith?" I asked.

The shot hit dead center. Not one muscle of his face moved, but in the very stillness of those dark features there was watchfulness and knowledge.

"Well, did you?" I pressed.

He shrugged. "In my work, I hear a great many names. It's possible that I may have heard that one, but I don't think so."

I fingered my drink for a moment. Then I said coldly, "You're lying, Mr. Lawrence. I don't know why you're doing it, but you're lying."

His tone was unbelievably sarcastic. "As long as you're calling me a liar, why don't you use my first name, Sydney?"

"Thank you, Domenic," I said equably, nibbling daintly at the olive from my martini.

Looking up blandly, I surprised in his eyes the first glint of humor I'd seen in him. We burst out laughing simultaneously.

The shared laughter lasted only a moment. Life was far too earnest, at that moment, for merriment. Our laughter had had in it, in fact, that note of hysteria which is closer to tears.

Suddenly his hand encircled mine in a viselike grip. I could feel the smooth glass pressing into my flesh, and I nearly cried out with pain and fear. But I gave him back look for look, and his dark gaze gave way first.

"Do you have a valid reason for believing Louise was murdered?" he asked quietly.

"I have a valid reason."

"Then why haven't you told the police?"

I said impatiently, "Let the police do their own job—they wouldn't believe me, anyway."

The silence between us seemed very long. The sounds of the Wheel—the voices, the sudden shrill bursts of laughter, and the clink of glasses, the soft, desultory ripple of piano music—were only an accompaniment to the unspoken words between us.

At last he spoke, reluctantly, as though the words were difficult to say, as though gentleness were torn out of him, instead of being freely given, "Sydney, please tell me whatever it is you know, or think you know, if only for your own safety's sake."

The freshly shaven jaw was already blue-black with the beginnings of a new beard, the mouth was narrowed against belief in me. I thought that I would rather have this dark, strong creature for ally than adversary.

I started then to tell him about the hidden room and the parcel of money, and the murderous car at Toronto. But I realized, with a sudden chill, that no one had absolved Domenic Lawrence of murder.

I stood up. "I really must be going," I said, my voice brittle with falsity.

"Go, then," he said disinterestedly, and slumped heavily against the leather cushions.

His words shut me out, and I felt oddly bereft as I walked away erectly, out of the Ferris Wheel, into the dark October night.

## 13

*It is the little rift within the lute
That by and by will make the music mute.*
—TENNYSON

On Monday morning I had to return to work. Dr. Alberti, the director of the conservatory, had been kind about a leave of absence during the week of Louise's death, but I knew that I must get back to my job.

On this weekday morning, everything seemed different; to rise and wash and dress and put on the kettle was strange. The shiny electric percolator sat there on the counter, mute testimony to Louise's absence, for she had taken coffee in the morning, and I tea. Going into the bathroom to get ready for work was somehow the most shattering experience, for there were Louise's toothbrush, her lipstick and eyebrow pencil, laid out on the big bathroom shelf, where the light was good; small, tangible evidences of the girl who had looked into this mirror and brushed her teeth and combed her hair before setting forth to be killed.

There was nothing new in the morning paper. The stories of Louise's murder were variations on the same theme, printed for the titillation of thrill-hungry readers, and to satisfy the public that the police department was moving in the case.

All during the past week, the papers had been full of the story, and they'd printed more than one blood-chilling photograph of Louise lying dead on the autumn leaves. There'd been interviews with Tony Ferris and with the dean of the conservatory, who pronounced Louise a "fine, serious girl with a real talent"; a report of the interrogation of Felix, who'd proved that he was at his meeting within minutes of picking up Louise; a picture of Felix, looking frightened and excited, and a bit guilty, actually, like those photos of men with shifty eyes who always turn out to be politicians or tax collectors.

I tossed this morning's paper aside and went out into the pungent morning air, to walk the short distance to the music school.

The old mansion which housed the Hoffman Conservatory presented an atmosphere far removed from violence. Built of mellowed gray stone, the conservatory once had been the home of Alfred Hoffman, a wealthy industrialist. An amateur musician of some enthusiasm, he had bequeathed his home and much of his fortune to the city, for the express purpose of founding a school which should be a memorial to him and a tribute to his muse.

I pushed open the heavy oak door and went in. The bright autumn sunshine streamed in through fresh white curtains; the polished floors shone with wax and sunlight. From the various practice rooms came the scraping sounds of a cello, a violin or two, and the clear, insistent notes of a flute, sweet and merry as a bird call. Someone, in one of the cubicles, was playing the piano violently, smashing away at the keys with brilliance and with fury.

I had a little office, blessedly mine alone. I let myself in and hung up my coat in the green metal cupboard. Taking a soft old rag from my lower desk drawer, I began to dust the few pieces of furniture and the single shelf of books. I opened the window to the cool October wind, and watched the white curtains stir into life in the morning sunshine.

I knew the small, diffident knock on the door could belong to only one person: Lucien King. He came in, bringing coffee in paper cups, and we sat sipping it together, neither of us saying much of consequence.

I noticed with pleasure, as I always did, the chiseled regularity of his features, the eyes deep-set, and the little-hurt-boy look; the lips, carved of soft red material, the black, wavy hair, the skin, just a subtle shade darker than another man's summer tan.

Unbidden, Louise's words spring into my mind: "So he's

a Negro—I certainly can't call him black. So what? Why does he have to be so damned conscious of it all the time? He never offers his hand first, when handshaking would be the natural thing to do. He's so aware of his color that he makes other people conscious of it, too."

Almost as though he read my mind, Lucien looked up and said, "The police had me in for questioning, Sydney. They kept asking me questions, because I worked with Louise at the Ferris Wheel." His tone was bitter. "They'd like it if I were the one, I suppose. Blacks are supposed to commit crimes of passion, aren't they?"

He crushed the paper cup and pitched it into the waste-basket. "Only, if your skin is dark, you're likely to use a knife or a razor, not pick someone off with a rifle."

"Lucien," I said in the calm, matter-of-fact way I'd learned to use in dealing with him, "no one suspects you of killing Louise. Felix Reichmann is white, and the police have had him in two or three times. They're questioning everyone who knew her at all well, I suppose. They've questioned me. It's routine procedure, so stop feeling sorry for yourself."

He dropped his head in his hands. "I know, Sydney. You don't have to tell me. That chip on my shoulder is so big you can see it a mile away, can't you? But I can't help it. I was born this way."

"You were born with a handicap, as the world still stands today," I said gently, "but God gave you a great talent to offset that handicap, so you've no choice but to overcome the one and develop the other."

He looked up at me in surprise, out of his opaque brown eyes. "I never heard you talk like that before, Sydney. I thought of you as rather—rather cold, I'm afraid."

I went over and stood at the window, my back to him. "Not cold, Lucien," I said carefully, "just sort of dead for a long time, just unaware of other people."

In a sudden burst of confidence, I added, "As a matter of fact, my father was a minister. I was brought up seeing life whole, seeing its marvelous pattern. I had—rather a bad time, a few months ago. I backslid for a while, I suppose."

He was studying me curiously. "You always have been something of a mystery woman, you know. I think this is the first time I've heard you mention your background."

It sent me off, his saying that, into a dream of sun and sea and sailboats, of a quiet, ordered, happy life beside the sea. I could see my father in his study, writing his Sunday sermon, and my mother, serene and smiling on the doorstep, as she watched me go off to school or a party. They had been so good, so much in love, yet so loving with me. I'd been almost glad one died so soon after the other. How could they have borne it without each other?

Then, just coming out of my grief, I'd met Jed and had fallen in love with him and married him. What had I known of him? He'd had a year at UCLA, and then had joined the Navy. Then he'd made a stab at Hollywood and had failed. When I'd met him, he'd been surfing on the beach, a young, suntanned god in navy-blue swim trunks, his hair several shades lighter than his skin, his eyes a glancing reflection of the blue ocean.

The students, in their varying styles of dress, were rushing up the broad walk now, hurrying to early classes. They all looked terribly alive, terribly eager, even the ones who pretended to be blasé and artistic and ultrasophisticated. They all looked a thousand years younger than I felt, even though many of them were older than I, chronologically.

Sighing, I turned back to Lucien. I was sad for him, weighted down as he was with the sorrows of an ancient race, but I had to ask him the question I meant to ask everyone whose life had touched Louise's.

"Lucien," I said casually, studying him under my lashes, "did you ever hear of Heather Smith?"

If he was playacting, it was good acting. He looked up questioningly. "I don't think so. Why?"

"It's just a name I heard," I said vaguely. "Lucien—has anyone been blackmailing you?"

He laughed, showing his white, white teeth, and slipped into the vernacular, which he did every now and again. "I got no money, girl. Who'd blackmail me?"

I wondered why Cecily hadn't told her lover about her blackmailer; it would have seemed the natural thing to do. Then I thought: He'd leave her, rather than have her risk losing Tina, rather than have her pay out her ex-husband's money to an extortionist; and Cecily couldn't bear that.

He was watching me. "I get the feeling you know something I don't," he said.

"I wish I did know something," I said soberly. "It's just suspicions I have, of course; nothing concrete." Except the manila envelope. That was real enough.

I broke off in mid-thought and looked at the door. The faintest sound, scarcely a real movement, had caught my ear. I looked at Lucien, and knew that he had heard it too. He was watching the door, and he stood up and moved, catlike, toward the paneled door.

Suddenly he flung it open, but there was no one there. The wide hall was deserted. White curtains eddying in the breeze were the only things moving in all the long hallway, although voices came from various classrooms, and the piano practice had resumed, the liquid notes of "Liebestraum" rippling from the keys with glib facility.

I looked down. Just inside my door, lying innocently on the beautiful old parquet floor which had been installed in the original mansion, was a folded note. I knew instantly that it was the mate to the note I'd found in my bag at the funeral home.

I picked it up and opened it reluctantly, conscious of Lucien's curious gaze.

> YOU'VE HAD ENOUGH WARNING, SYDNEY MACKENZIE. FORGET LOUISE. GO BACK TO CALIFORNIA, OR YOU'LL BE SORRY.

The paper was cheap white typing stock, the words and letters cut from magazines and newspapers. I knew without doubt that there would be no fingerprints. The murderer— I had begun to think of Heather as a murderer, I realized— was far too slick and clever to leave anything so incriminating as fingerprints.

"What's wrong?" Lucien asked.

I shook my head. I wasn't ready yet to reveal my name to this man, of whom I knew very little, after all.

He shrugged. "Well, I'd better get to my vocal class. Professor Harrison is a fanatic about promptness." He picked up his music case and gave my shoulder a quick, consoling squeeze, which touched me deeply, for it was the only time he had ever touched me, except for a brief handshake when we were introduced.

"Don't worry, Sydney. It was nothing. People are snoopy. It only means someone is interested in murder, and knows you were Louise's friend."

But I wasn't convinced, and neither, I thought, was he. The same thought must inevitably have occurred to both of us: someone, student or teacher, at Hoffman Conservatory, was after me. The chase was narrowing down.

On a sudden impulse, after Lucien had left, I walked down the nearly deserted corridors, studying every face for its possible hidden guilt. No one looked sinister, no one looked particularly interested in me. I knew some of the faces, but no one was especially familiar to me.

It was a few minutes before I realized what had been at the back of my mind: I wanted to see who had been playing "Liebestraum" and then had stopped so abruptly—and had begun again, so shortly after the evil little note had been slipped under my door.

Notebook in hand, as though I were looking for someone in particular, I peeped into the practice rooms. Half of them were empty at this hour; the students were in classes. In one, however, Mikhail Dubrocek was practicing the fingering of his violin. He turned his beautiful, dreamy smile on me for a moment, then went on with his practice. In another, Selena Hancock, the harpist, would have engaged me in one of her marathon conversations, but I murmured something about a telephone message, and backed out hastily. Selena had been known to corner an unwary victim and talk straight through appointments, rehearsals, and class beginnings.

In the cubicle at the far end of the hall, cigarette smoke still lingered on the air, and a cigarette stub smoldered in the ash-darkened copper tray. The music of "Liebestraum" still lay open on the piano, and I could not rid myself of the feeling that the skillful rippling music, played with expertise but without emotion, had been a taunt. Heather Smith, perhaps, thumbing her nose at me and my amateur detection?

## 14

*It is a little picture painted well.*
—RICHARD W. GILDER

Through the open office door, the soft plink-plink of a harp's strings mingled with the harsher syncopation of my electric typewriter as I finished the last letter before lunch.

Someone came in the open office door and approached my desk. I looked up, bewildered, to see Domenic Lawrence, beautifully groomed and attractive as always, his elegant features, as always, showing nothing more revealing than polite disinterest.

"Can I help you?" I asked, my hands still resting on the typewriter keys.

"Perhaps. I just wanted to ask you something."

"Yes?" I waited while he appeared to deliberate.

"Is there somewhere we could go for lunch?"

I hesitated. "I had planned to eat a sandwich in the park and go on to the sidewalk art show."

He looked briefly amused, then asked amiably, "May I join you, then? I'll buy the sandwiches."

I smiled reluctantly, then took my handbag from the desk drawer. "All right, come along. I have to be back at one."

He helped me with the suede jacket which was exactly what the autumn day demanded, and we walked down the wide corridor and out the front door of the Hoffman Conservatory.

Outside he hesitated. "Would it be easier to drive to the park, or would you rather have lunch in a restaurant?"

I shook my head. "Let's walk. It's not far, and we can get a sandwich at Primo's, on the way."

We walked briskly in the clear nip of autumn air, and I

gave him little covert glances whenever he threw a sentence my way. "Elegance" was the best word to describe him, I decided, elegance in the Old World sense. He was like the Laughing Cavalier, or perhaps a portrait by Van Dyke, dashing and refined, with a sort of leashed virility. I didn't know what to make of him. I thought that he distrusted me, yet he had sought out my company, whatever his reason.

"What kind of sandwich would you like?" he asked, cozy as a husband, and I said, "Roast beef with hot mustard, please."

We went under the dirty red-and-white-striped awning into Primo's, where everyone at the conservatory went for sandwiches and coffee. The short, squat Giovanni Primo, who spoke the most guttural of English after fifty years in this country, had been serving the students at Hoffman for the past thirty-five years. He looked like Mussolini—bold, powerful, granite-faced—but he was jovial as a circus clown, accepting good-naturedly the jokes and jibes of the Hoffman boys. He did little actual work himself these days, but he was an expert at extracting top performances from the youngest and least experienced of his employees.

He greeted me respectfully. " 'Allo, Miss Webster. How you feeling now?"

"I'm fine, thank you, Giovanni."

After reading the newspaper accounts of Louise's death, he had commiserated with me tearfully, and even now he behaved as though I were just recovering from some near-fatal illness.

I was surprised when he greeted Domenic enthusiastically. "Mr. Lawrence! It's good to see you back again. Did you get to Napoli?"

Domenic grinned. "I kissed the soil in your honor, Giovanni. Will you be going over yourself next year?"

Giovanni sighed. "If the taxes permit." He rolled his beady eyes. "Such income tax."

"You'll get no sympathy from me," Domenic said serenely. "Such income!"

While our sandwiches were being made by the counter

girl, Domenic and Giovanni talked along in an easy, joking fashion, which rather surprised me. I had forgotten there must be another, more verbal Domenic Lawrence, a man who had long, discursive luncheons with other attorneys, a man who prepared briefs and went to court; in short, another man from the one who had mourned the death of Louise, a different man from the brooding, superior, dark-browed creature who had seemed my silent accuser.

We took our sandwiches and our cardboard cartons of hot coffee into the little park and sat on a bench, talking a little, watching the fat pigeons and the glorious autumn leaves. In the center, in a cement hexagon, a squat marble fountain sent torrents of crystal water into the air, attracting three or four sparrows, who bathed lazily along its marble rim.

"I thought I'd never come here again," I said, brushing the crumbs off my skirt for the pigeons who waited for them, at a safe distance. "But it's still beautiful, isn't it?"

He looked at me for a moment before answering. "Yes, Louise is gone, but the trees are here, and the birds and the sun—all the eternal things. It's only we who are ephemeral."

"No," I said stubbornly, and it was a measure of my recovery that I was able to speak in the words of my father. "We only seem ephemeral. But everything changes, even the leaves turn to dust; yet nothing is lost, not the leaves, not us."

There was a long silence, then he said, as though I'd just spoken, "I know. But death tends to make you forget that fact of nature. We know the caterpillar will emerge as a butterfly. We don't know what will become of us."

I thought of Jed. "Something better and more beautiful, like the butterfly," I said.

We got up from the green wooden bench and put our sandwich wrappers and empty cartons into the big yellow wire trash container. Despite the midday sunshine, there was a bit of autumn chill in the air now, and the red and green leaves were whirling down in little torrents, presaging the beginning of winter. I shivered a little, thinking of Louise as I had seen her last, a lonely figure lying in the rain, skewered by the bright police spotlight.

"We'll just have time for the curbstone show, if we hurry a bit," Domenic said, looking at his watch.

We walked briskly toward the business district, where a few city blocks were displaying the work of local artists. The exhibit was usually held in September, according to one of the girls at the conservatory, but there had been a calendar conflict, and surprisingly, the show had been blessed with this unusual blue-and-golden weather.

I was looking forward to it. Once I had had painting ambitions of my own, but I had come to realize that my gift was a small one, and I'd given it up. In any case, I had thought, in those days, that I would be housewife and mother, and happy in that job.

I drew back from the thought and said to Domenic Lawrence, "You said you wanted to see me about something?"

He hesitated, then shook his head. "Not just now. This is too beautiful, isn't it?"

Too beautiful to spoil. The words hung unspoken on the wine of autumn air, but I was too bemused by the wonder of the day to question him.

The downtown streets were gay with color. Along the curbstones, on temporary display frames, and on lengths of clothesline, hung dozens and dozens of oil paintings and watercolors and etchings. Artists, some diffident, some openly solicitous of business, were stationed beside their own work. It was all bright and amusing and gay, and I found my spirits lifting.

We looked at all of them as carefully as my waning lunch hour would allow. Domenic was surprisingly knowledgeable about art, and I found myself listening attentively to what he had to say.

"You know something about painting," he said keenly at one point.

"A little. I studied for a while."

I was staring at a particularly lovely seascape. I smiled at the artist, a middle-aged woman with a pitted, weather-beaten face and long red hair bound back by a broad white band. "It's Carmel, isn't it?"

She smiled, delighted at my recognition. "Yes. Do you know Carmel?"

"I was brought up in Monterey, and of course I've been to Carmel hundreds of times."

She said wistfully, "I'd like to live there and paint it over and over again, as Andrew Wyeth does Chadds Ford. I'd never grow tired of it."

"Your painting is so lovely," I said. "You've done the sad, windblown cypresses so well."

I saw the price tag up in the corner. Thirty dollars. I longed to own the little painting, with its marvelous blues and greens and grays, but I knew that I had something like seven dollars in my purse, and that it must last until payday.

"Let me buy it for you," Domenic said, as though reading my mind.

I said quickly, uncomfortably, "Oh, no, I couldn't. But thank you, anyway."

He said firmly to the woman, "We'll take it," and took his billfold from his pocket. Smiling, he added, "You wouldn't deprive this charming lady of a sale, surely?"

Half-reluctantly, I smiled back. It seemed we had declared a truce, here in this Greenwich Village atmosphere, with the October sun pouring down on the artists and the paintings, on the smiling shoppers who paused to look and admire.

Her cheeks red with gratification, the woman wrapped the painting carefully in brown paper and tied a string around it. I thanked her, and as we walked away, turned to thank Domenic.

"It's far too extravagant a present, but I do thank you. It's a wonderful picture, and the scene takes me straight back to childhood. I spent many hours on the beach at Carmel. I remember we used to buy huge black cherries and sit eating them on the white sands, with the dark-red juice running down our chins."

I smiled in reminiscence, and he said, " 'We' being your family, I suppose."

"There were only three of us—Mother, Daddy, and I—

but we were complete. It was a wonderful time."

He looked as though he planned to ask more, and I was half-sorry I'd spoken, but we came then to a portrait, just a head, of a girl with blond hair framing her face, a square jawline, an unsmiling mouth. Her eyes, cool and knowledgeable, looked out at me. I stopped in front of the picture, and I couldn't hold back the words. "She's very like Louise," I said.

He stood there for a moment. "Yes. Very like," he said.

"I wonder what she was really like underneath," I mused.

He shot me a quick, sharp glance. "What do you mean by that?"

"I wish you wouldn't pounce so," I answered, nettled. "I was just remembering what she said to me one day. She said, 'Sydney, doesn't life sometimes seem completely useless, completely empty?'"

"Not the words of a happy woman, in love with a man, eager to marry him, would you say?" His voice was detached, but I could feel the pain beneath the coolness.

I said gently, "She could have loved you and still have had unresolved conflicts from childhood."

"Now you talk like a psychology textbook," he said impatiently.

"Well, we're all case histories, aren't we?"

He shrugged, and once again I noted the severity of his lips, the firm, resolute lips of a man who held no brief for weakness. I could see him, fifteen or twenty years from now, in the black robes of a judge, pronouncing sentence upon a prisoner, with complete justice, and perhaps a little mercy, but without bending. I wondered what he would think of a man like Jed, a man who had taken the easy way through life and the easy way out of it.

"Is something wrong?"

With a start of dismay, I realized that he had been studying my face. "Nothing," I said, but I could feel the color rising and rising in my cheekbones, as though somehow he could read my mind.

"Well!" said a familiar voice. "I didn't realize you two

knew each other." It was Cecily, impossibly elegant, as always, in a smart suit in the newest shade of gray. "Playing hooky, Sydney?"

I looked at my watch. "I should be back now."

Domenic looked down at her with the indulgent smile most men awarded the dainty, diminutive Cecily. "Nice to see you, Cecily."

She couldn't resist flirting. "I'm in the book, Nicky. Why haven't you called me? I've been waiting to hear what you've found out about—that little matter."

Why should I care that his face seemed to harden, that he took her off to one side for a moment and murmured to her? But I did.

"I'd better go back," I said when they turned back to me. "I'm going to be late, as it is. Why don't you two stay and look at the other paintings?"

"Nonsense," he said shortly. "I'll walk back with you, or we can hail a cab, if we can find one."

"Walking's faster," I said. His manner had changed so swiftly, not, I thought, because of Cecily's presence, but because she had reminded him of something. I felt once again his cold dislike of me, and it puzzled as well as hurt. Only a few minutes ago he had liked me, felt warmly toward me.

"I have a class," Cecily said. "I'll go along with you."

Her quick eye had caught sight of the package under Domenic's arm. "Did you buy a painting?" she asked inquisitively.

"It's Sydney's," he said. "A seascape."

She looked at me quickly, but did not press the matter; yet somehow I knew she had guessed it was a gift from Domenic. I think it angered her, the idea that an attractive man like Domenic had been buying gifts for quiet, repressed Sydney. She was infatuated with Lucien, but Cecily was constitutionally unable to endure lack of attention from any man.

All the way back to Hoffman Conservatory, she flirted with Domenic, elbowing me out of the conversation, and not too subtly at that. At first I was amused, and then I began to feel the faint, healthy stirring of anger. Watching her murmur to Domenic, so that he had to bend his head down to hear her, seeing the provocative little looks she flashed up at him, I was carried back to girlhood and the teen-age boy I'd brought triumphantly back to my side, after the class sex symbol had tried to snare him. Nothing, after all, so brings out the essential female in a woman as watching another woman try to seize her man.

That brought me up short. By what complicated process of rationalization had I come to consider Domenic Lawrence my property? He had been in love with Louise, that was irrefutable; and at this moment, he was giving Cecily that amused, indulgent look which means a man finds a woman attractive. For me he had shown little other than hostility and suspicion. He bought you a rather special gift, the other, optimistic part of my brain said gleefully. It was a whim, a momentary kindness, I reminded myself. It meant nothing.

We were back at Hoffman now, and Cecily leaned against Domenic ever so slightly, laughing deliciously. "Call me soon, Nicky. Remember, I'm a client now."

"I will." But the word "client" seemed to have put a damper on his good spirits, because he scowled in his old, impatient way.

Turning to me, he said briefly, "I enjoyed the art show. Thank you for taking me along."

"But what was it you wanted to see me about?" I asked.

He hesitated. "It was—business," he said somberly. "I'll call you about it." He looked away from my face as though he had remembered something loathsome about me.

"Good-bye," he said, and walked away abruptly.

I could not understand him. He had sought out my company and had seemed to enjoy it. Once or twice, as though forgetting his grief over Louise for the moment, he had broken into reluctant laughter over some spontaneous comment of mine, and I, in turn, had laughed and felt carefree for the first time in more than a year.

Cecily looked after his tall, rugged figure and smiled her

little Cheshire-cat smile. "I suppose he's still mourning for Louise, but I wonder if he's not ripe for someone else about now."

Her glance flicked over me and found me wanting. "He bought you a painting? You must have broken the ice."

I pushed open the big door, and we stepped from sunshine into shadow. "It was just an impulse," I said, "a kindness on his part, because I said I had grown up in Monterey."

Too late I saw the curiosity leaking out of her eyes. "You never say anything about yourself." She waited.

I tried to smile. "Nothing to say, I guess."

I looked at my watch and said, "It's ten past one, Cecily. I'm late. See you."

I hung up my jacket in the little closet and went back to the dull safety of the electric typewriter, the file cabinets, and the telephone. Through the welter of letters and file cards and student records, the memory of the golden noon hour filtered. It had been fun, and something else besides. From time to time I glanced at the brown-paper parcel which lay on the table opposite me. It was precious to me; I refused to decide whether it was the picture itself—which had evoked happy memories—or the very fact of the gift itself.

It was nothing, just the light, meaningless kindness of an affluent man, I told myself. But I longed to open the package, to hold the painting in my hands, to get from the very touch of it that sensation of the giver, that psychic force which, everyone knows, just precedes falling in love.

I came to myself with a start. Love! I had had all I needed of love and sorrow. Love would have to wait a few more years, if it ever came again. Perhaps then I could find someone solid and stable, certainly not someone like Domenic Lawrence, a man still in love with another woman.

I clacked away determinedly at the keys of the typewriter, turning my thoughts resolutely toward the list of performers for next Friday night's performance in Hoffman Hall. Cecily's name was on the list. She was working for her master's degree in piano, and this public recital was one of the most important requirements. The only other name I really recognized was that of Barbara Carmichael, the girl who had found Louise in the park. I shuddered. If her name made me think of that wild, rainy night, what must it be like for Barbara, remembering Louise's body as she and her fiancé stumbled on it?

The phone rang and I picked it up. "Hoffman Conservatory."

"Sydney?"

I answered, "Yes," automatically, and then could have bitten my tongue. It was the same evil whisper, the same sexless voice, which had called me at home.

"What do you want?" I cried angrily.

"I want you to go back home, Sydney, back to California, before you get into really deep trouble. Wouldn't it be embarrassing to have your friends know about your husband, Mrs. MacKenzie?"

The snide, sadistic tenor of the words infuriated me. He was so craven, this Voice, so cowardly, so cruel. I wanted to see the Face, to strike back.

"I'm not afraid of you!" I cried. "I'll tell people myself, if I must. I'm not responsible for someone else's sins." Saying the words made them true, suddenly. I had no really close friends in Newton. Those people I had begun to know would not shun me because my husband had committed robbery and had run away. And I was competent at my job; I needn't fear losing it.

"Sydney," said the Voice insistently, "you're tempting fate by staying in Newton. Go back to California, where you belong. Or would you like to join your friend Louise?"

"Forget it," I said coldly. "I'm not leaving Newton. I like it here." And I hung up.

But I found I was trembling. All the primitive terror of the unknown seemed to have seized upon me. If I'd met a madman in a dark alley, I could have screamed and run, but this person had no body, no face, and I could not fight him.

I went back to work, but my hands shook on the keys, and

the memory of that hour in the wind and sun with Domenic Lawrence no longer seemed like a hidden talisman. For all I knew, *he* might be the thin, disguised voice on the telephone. In all the world, it seemed, there was no one left whom I could trust.

## 15

*Write her fair words still in foulest letters.*
—SHAKESPEARE

Later in the afternoon, as I was passing through the hallway with an armload of sheet music to return to the school
library, I met Phil Valenti.

He stopped me with a hand on my arm. "Irene told me
to bring you home to supper, if you're not busy tonight,"
he said. "She thinks it's not good for you to be alone in that
house. Can you come?"

"I'd love to."

People were very kind, I thought, as I watched him hurry
down the hall. Jed had spoiled me for all people for so long,
yet here were half-strangers, like Phil and Irene, going out
of their way to ease my fright and loneliness.

At five o'clock I tidied up my desk and put on my coat.
Phil was lounging outside my office door. He was short and
stocky, with curly black hair, and he and Irene made an
oddly assorted couple; but there was something very appealing about his broad peasant face.

"My ancient chariot awaits," he said.

"Oh, Phil . . . I hope you haven't been waiting long. I
completely forgot to tell you this afternoon . . . I'm driving
Louise's car."

He looked faintly surprised, and I said, feeling a little
uncomfortable, "It seems she left it to me in her will. I feel
very odd about taking it, because she must have had closer
friends. But meantime, I can't deny it's very convenient to
have."

"She was a strange girl, Louise." He walked to the exit
with me and pushed the brass bar which opened the door.

"In spite of her love of good company, I don't think she felt close to many people, and she had no relatives left. She liked you, I know that, so if she wanted you to have her car, why shouldn't you accept it?"

He gave me their address and directions for finding the house, and I followed his car as closely as I could, winding through the rush-hour traffic, until we reached a residential section on the western side of the city. It was a large, rambling gray house, one of many old mansions which had been converted into apartments, and somehow not the sort of place in which one would have pictured Irene. One expected her cool beauty, her spectacular red hair, to emerge from a very modern, very expensive luxury apartment.

I was a little touched, when we entered the apartment, to have her greet me with genuine warmth and concern. She was so single-minded in her devotion to Phil that I scarcely expected her to be aware of other people.

"You look exhausted, Sydney," she said. "Come and have a drink. The dinner's almost ready."

I sank down gratefully on a shabby, wonderfully comfortable sofa and looked around me. The place, more studio than apartment, fitted Phil better than it did Irene, I thought. A tiny kitchen and, presumably, a bedroom and bath opened off the vast living room, with its clutter of paperback books, its white-painted Franklin stove, and the weather-pitted statue of Pan, surrounded by ferns, which dominated the bay windows at the front.

There was a really lovely spinet piano at one end of the room, and Phil's violin case lay on top of this. In every bit of spare space not covered by paperbacks, there was sheet music. The total effect was one of organized disorder and somehow completely charming.

"I love your apartment," I said to Irene.

She seemed pleased. "I decided there was no use in trying to make these high ceilings and vast rooms look modern, so I simply furnished it with a conglomeration of things we both liked."

Phil brought wine—New York State table wine—and we

drank that while the sauce was heating and water was boiling for the spaghetti. After that we had dinner: the spaghetti with Irene's gourmet sauce, crusty hot garlic bread, and a wonderful salad with dressing mixed carefully by Phil. It was all simple and homey and unpretentious, and I felt curiously relaxed and happy.

The conversation was good, and after a while Phil played the violin and Irene accompanied him. I watched, fascinated, as he tucked his chin into the wood of the fiddle and nodded his head very slightly at Irene. I watched her face, beautiful as a queen's, submissive as a slave's, as she followed the flashing bow, the flying fingers. I had forgotten that such love could exist, could carry on in a world which I had come to consider full of hate.

Finally we had big cups of black coffee and some sort of exotic Italian dessert, compounded of brandy-soaked cake and apricot jam and whipped cream. I knew that I should be going; we all had to get up early in the morning, but I was reluctant to leave the sanctuary of this shabby, delightful flat.

"Wonderful," I said, leaning back against the shabby, comfortable couch. "This is the best evening I've had since I came to Newton."

Instantly I regretted my comment. Irene looked at me oddly, and Phil gave me a glance of sympathy which made me acutely uncomfortable. I do not like pity. In that one quick look from his dark eyes, I saw compassion for my loneliness, and an awareness of my estrangement from life.

To cover, to protect my vulnerability, I said hastily, "Irene—Phil—please forgive me for asking a presumptuous question, but I think it's terribly important. Are you being blackmailed?"

Irene's pearly white skin turned paler than ever, and Phil's kindly gaze changed quickly to one of anger.

"Where exactly did you get that idea?" Irene asked, her tone completely hostile.

I felt I had betrayed their hospitality, so generously extended, yet I had to go on. I got up and picked up my bag

from the floor, where I'd dropped it. I took out the Xeroxed
copy of lines from the Seattle city directory. "Valenti, Philip
(Maria) . . . 116 South Elm . . . Tchr."

"You *are* from Seattle?" I said to Phil.

He glanced at the paper but did not answer. I looked at
Irene, and I knew that she could kill me, quite simply and
unerringly, without a single qualm.

"What are you trying to do?" she demanded. Her nostrils
had turned white with anger.

I shook my head. "I'm not trying to do anything, Irene.
It's what I believe someone else is trying to do. *Are* you
being blackmailed?"

Phil was very quiet. "It's all right," he said to Irene. "She
wouldn't tip her hand if she were the one. Let's all sit down
and talk."

Irene perched on the arm of a chair, but her back was
still stiff, her beautiful eyes blazing. I felt that I had made an
implacable enemy, unless I could convince her of my ab-
solute sincerity.

"Look," I said, "I'm not trying to pry secrets from either
of you. It's obvious you've been married before, Phil, and
have concealed that fact, for reasons of your own. That copy
from the city directory was in one of several envelopes I
found the other day. Some of the material is far more
flammable than that, and I know of at least two people who
have been paying blackmail money." I hesitated. "One was
Louise. And she was killed."

I had often thought of Irene as a tigress defending her
cub, and that's exactly the way she looked now, her beautiful
face suffused with fear, her eyes black with anger.

"You see," she said in a low voice, "we must keep on
paying, Phil, forever, if necessary. I don't care about the
money. I just care about you. I want you alive."

He smiled at her in a moment of such complete intimacy
that I felt embarrassed at being there at all. They were a
closed corporation, needing no outsiders, sufficient unto
themselves. Their communication was wordless and complete, and I wanted to cry with envy.

Phil turned to me and said, "We have something to show you."

He went to the desk, unlocked a drawer, and took a letter from it.

The envelope was a plain, dime-store business envelope. Inside was a familiar sheet of plain white typing paper, also dime-store variety. The note, like the one I had found in my bag at the funeral parlor, was constructed from newspaper and magazine type: REMEMBER WHAT HAPPENED TO LOUISE ALBRIGHT. IF YOU DON'T PAY ON YOUR ACCOUNT, IT WILL HAPPEN TO ONE OF YOU.

I looked at them squarely. "You are being blackmailed, then?"

"Why do you think we live here?" Irene said, her tone bitter. "In this place with the paint peeling and no closets and a kitchenette the size of a doll's-house kitchen? Phil earns a good salary. Our friend, as he signs himself so often, takes a very sizable amount of money every three months. When we don't pay, we get threatened. But this is the most explicit threat we've had. The other letters only threatened exposure."

I waited in the silence, and finally Irene lifted her head proudly. "Phil and I aren't married, you see, we're just living together. His wife won't give him a divorce." She added defiantly, "I don't care, really. I would flaunt our arrangement in front of the whole world, if necessary. But stately old schools like Hoffman take a dim view of our sort of relationship. Phil would lose his job, and it's very important to him."

"How did it start—the blackmailing?" I ventured.

"Soon after we came to Newton," Phil said, "we received a letter, taunting us about my legal marriage and asking for money. Otherwise, the writer said, he'd betray us."

"He's been bleeding us," Irene said, her fingers drumming furiously on the chair arm. "Every time we get angry and hold up the payment, we get an absolutely terrifying letter. But this"—she gestured at the letter I held—"is an out-and-out threat of murder." She shuddered. "There isn't the least question in my mind that he—or she—means it."

"Nor mine," I said bleakly. "There's Louise's death to prove it." Making a sudden, unthinking decision, I confessed, "I haven't had any demands for money, but I have been ordered to leave town. Someone obviously knows my secret, too."

They regarded me, both politely silent, until I forced myself to continue. "You know that I'm from California, but you don't know that I was married, very briefly, and that my husband was—Jed was—he committed a robbery, and a night watchman was shot. I had no inkling, we were so happy. We were sitting in a little restaurant on Fisherman's Wharf, when the police came to question him. He was shot later, trying to escape from them."

I saw their horror and their sympathy, and I girded myself against it. "I changed my name and came east, but there were newspaper pictures in the West Coast papers. My father was a minister and well known; it was human interest to the newspapers. Someone recognized me from one of the pictures, I suppose. Even Louise did—she said so in her last letter to me—but she was too kind to mention it to me when she was alive."

I told them, then, about the parcel of money I'd found, about my trip to Toronto, my belief that Louise had been killed by the blackmailer.

"Then why," Irene mused, "did she have that money addressed, ready to mail? I mean, if she was about to pay, why should they kill her?"

I shook my head. "I can only think that she had changed her mind, or was late with the payment, or perhaps had simply told the blackmailer, when he called, that she didn't intend to pay. Louise wasn't a weak person. If she had made up her mind not to mail the money, I think she'd have stuck with the decision. And I don't suppose we'll ever know, now, for what reason she was being blackmailed."

We talked for a while longer, worrying the whole thing as a dog worries a bone, but we came up with nothing new. Finally, guiltily, I got to my feet.

"Tomorrow is a working day. I'm sorry I've stayed so late."

"It was good for both of us," Phil said. "We needed to talk to someone."

Unexpectedly, Irene touched my arm lightly and said, "Will you come again very soon?"

The crust of ice inside me was beginning to melt. "I'd love to," I said.

Then, as they walked with me to the door, I added, troubled, "What are you going to do about the blackmail money?"

"Pay, damn it, pay!" Irene said, her magnificent eyes flashing. "But I don't mind telling you, if I knew who was doing this, I would kill him with my bare hands." She looked proudly at Phil. "He's a great man, and a very good one. I would do anything on earth to shield him from unhappiness."

Going out into the chilly night, climbing into my dead friend's little car, I shuddered as I remembered Irene's parting words. She would be relentless in her pursuit of anyone who harmed Phil, and I knew that I would hate to be at the receiving end of that deep and bitter hatred.

# 16

*. . . a little sunny and a little sad, like the season.*
—Henry Brooks Adams

When I fitted the key into the lock, I could hear the telephone ringing. I hurried inside and picked up the receiver.
It was Domenic Lawrence, sounding cross, and underneath
the crossness, a little worried, I thought.

"I've been calling all evening," he said. "I thought something might be wrong."

"I haven't been murdered, if that's what you mean," I
said, my voice cool. "I was out for the evening."

"Oh. I seem to remember Louise writing me that her
roommate never went out."

"Then I've changed, haven't I?"

There was a little silence at the other end of the phone,
then he said, his voice sounding almost reluctant, "I thought
perhaps you might have dinner with me on Saturday night.
It must be difficult for you, not to say dangerous, living
there by yourself."

My pleasure at being protected and cherished was mixed
with suspicion: first Phil and Irene, and now Domenic, had
made themselves responsible for my welfare. Part of me felt
grateful, but the other part was distrustful of all of them.

But I said yes.

Saturday itself turned out to be an Indian-summer day:
blue skies, white clouds, amber sunlight. In the afternoon,
all my household tasks done, I washed my hair and took a
towel and a book and a pot of tea out into the garden.
Thomas went with me, and with fine feline showmanship,
ran up the peach tree, sharpened his claws wildly, and settled

down on a wide bough, to sleep in the sunlight, his great paws hanging languidly in the air.

There was a heady smell of grapes from Miss Grimes's little arbor, and I reached up and pulled a bunch of silvered blue fruit from its hiding place among the thick leaves.

I sat there with a sweater around my shoulders against the slight autumn chill and toweled my hair and sucked the grapes. Once again I felt a sense of restoration, of revitalized life. The sun's warmth, the wild, extravagant colors of the autumn flowers, the ivy turning crimson on the wall, were all signs of nature's constant renewal, and a kind of promise for me.

I pulled from my pocket an unopened letter from my absent landlady, Miss Grimes—the first personal letter I had received from anyone since moving to 1 Greenwood Place. It began with her characteristic enthusiasm and keenness. She was enjoying Europe, except for the water and the poor-quality paper napkins. It was delightful, after all these years of teaching, of adhering to a strict schedule, to feel young and carefree again.

Then she added, "I have asked my nephew to turn over the key of the house to you. I gave it to him when he was in college, and his parents were traveling, and he has never sent it back to me. I'm afraid it might make you uneasy, if you knew that someone else could enter your home."

There in the stillness of Miss Grimes's garden, I laughed aloud, a little hysterically. Darling Miss Grimes, I thought, the fact that your bad little nephew might have access to 1 Greenwood Place is as nothing beside the things which have been happening in Newton lately.

I wondered if I should go and get my notepaper and write to her about Louise's murder, or if she would be terribly distressed and want to rush home to exorcise the evil from her lovely house.

The whir of the front doorbell finally penetrated my consciousness, and I got to my feet, muttering, "Damn!" I twisted the towel turban-style around my still-damp hair and went to answer.

My caller was, to my barely concealed astonishment, Felix Reichmann, looking somehow less youthful today, despite his round face and ruddy cheeks. He looked now— and probably always would look—like a middle-aged boy.

"Hello, Sydney," he said. "Forgive me for coming unannounced, but I was in the neighborhood and I felt the need of company."

I held the door wider. "Come on in. I've been sitting in the garden; it's lovely and sunny out there. Would you like a cup of coffee or tea?"

"Tea, please, if it's not too much trouble."

I made fresh tea, and he carried the tray out into the sunlit garden. I could see that he wanted to talk.

"Beautiful house, Sydney," he said. "How did you manage to find it?"

"I answered a want ad, shortly after I came to Newton. I was living at the YWCA and had just gotten myself the job at Hoffman, and I wanted to be on my own. This place was so perfect, I could hardly believe my good luck when Miss Grimes agreed to rent it to me at a price I could almost afford! I think she liked me and sensed how much I liked the house, so she let me have it. She's a darling woman. She's traveling in Europe now, with an elderly cousin, and they're both happy as larks. I had a letter from her today, from Vienna. They've just toured every castle in Germany, I should think."

He set his cup down carefully. "And Louise? I don't think I ever knew how you met Louise."

"I didn't really want to share the house," I confessed now, "but it wasn't easy, getting along on my salary. I needed someone to share expenses, and fortunately for me, Louise answered my ad and we took a liking to each other."

He said suddenly, as though he hadn't really been listening to me, "If the police call me in again, I'm going to insist on taking a lie-detector test. I have the feeling they didn't quite believe me about the time I arrived at the meeting, the night Louise was killed. The police are doubters—have to be, I suppose."

"What do you think will happen with the investigation?" I asked curiously.

He shrugged. "I think they'll chalk it up to a teen-age sniper, someone who didn't really mean to kill anyone." He paused. "And it may very well have happened that way."

I shook my head. "No, I think it was murder, Felix."

In the act of lighting his pipe, cupping it against the wind, he paused and looked at me. "You feel it was murder?"

"Yes."

He finished lighting the pipe, and the fragrance of tobacco mingled with the scent of sunshine and chrysanthemums. "That's a large statement."

"I know."

There was a long silence, but he didn't belabor the point. It was as though he were waiting for me to make a statement at my own leisure.

He looked straight at me, his boyish face set in stern, unhappy lines. "People are seldom killed without reason, would you say? There must have been some secret in her life, something which made her a candidate for murder." He gestured toward the teapot. "May I have another cup of that, Sydney?"

"Of course." While I poured it for him, added the lemon and the sugar, I considered the feasibility of my next words.

And finally I uttered them. "What would you say to blackmail?"

The stubby, childlike lashes flew up, and he looked at me, his face naked with fear. "Blackmail? What do you mean?"

I avoided looking at him. "I think Louise was being blackmailed about something, and that she was killed because she wouldn't pay up."

I poured my own tea and sipped it before he answered slowly, "That would make sense, wouldn't it?"

"She wasn't the only person at Hoffman who was being blackmailed."

He looked straight at me at last. "You?"

"I have something to hide. I suppose everyone has something to hide. I haven't received any demands for money as yet, but I've been warned to leave town or have my secret told. And—I know that two or three others have been paying hush money."

He got up and began to walk restlessly about the garden, his feet heedless of Miss Grimes's herbaceous borders, her autumn flowers. My hands were trembling. I had begun to realize that, sooner or later, I might reveal my knowledge to the wrong person—to the blackmailer, not the blackmailed. Then I would become a candidate for murder myself.

But I had to know. I said, "Please try to understand why I'm asking this, Felix. It's not prying, believe me."

A frown was gathering on his baby face, and I hastened on. "I found a typed dossier on you." I swallowed. "It said you had been a member of the Communist party some years ago."

There was a long silence. Then, "It's not the sort of thing you can keep quiet, is it?" he said. "I should never have paid the first time; I see that now. The smart thing would have been to refuse to pay and let the blackmailer tell the whole story, if he wanted to. I wonder if leeches like that ever do tell, when they're not paid. I wonder if it isn't their stock in trade—pretending they'd reveal all, if they didn't get what they wanted."

I said gently, "Don't tell me anything you don't want to, Felix. For all you know, I may be your blackmailer."

He shook his head and said glumly, "No, it started months before you arrived in Newton. If I weren't a bachelor, it would cramp my style considerably, paying out that fifty bucks a month. But it seemed cheaper than to take a chance on losing my job. Hoffman is one of the best schools in the country, and also one of the most conservative. If I lost my job here under suspicious circumstances, where could I hope to get another as good?"

There was another of his long silences; then he said, "When I was much younger, when I was in college, I did something very foolish. I became a card-carrying Communist. It lasted about two years; then I was fed up and disillusioned, and I quit and forgot about it. I didn't think anyone knew, except one or two old friends, and I simply put it out of my mind. But someone ferreted it out and started sending me those hellish letters. When I received the first one and didn't pay, I got another letter, threatening not only to report to the dean that I was once a subversive, but also to hint in the proper quarters that I'm a bachelor because I'm a homosexual." He looked squarely at me. "It's not true, but that's the sort of story which can be spread around and ruin a man's life and his work." He shrugged despondently. "So I paid."

I felt ashamed. Ever since they had taken Jed away and killed him when he tried to run, I had been absorbed in self-pity; nothing else could touch me but my grief and my disillusionment. Yet all around me there were problems, there was misery, which I had been too blind and selfish to see.

"What do you know about Louise?" I asked finally, out of a silence. "It's hard to imagine her submitting to blackmail, but this person seems to have done an expert job of dredging up the really painful things in each person's life."

He shook his head. "She wasn't one to talk about herself; she liked to discuss ideas and books and music. I know she came from Chicago and that she used to live with an elderly aunt and uncle, but both had died. I always thought of her as a rather solitary person."

There was a long silence. Then, "I'd like to have that material, Sydney," he said. "I've been paying money for that dead horse for quite a time now."

I hesitated. "I think I'd better hang onto it, Felix. It's evidence of Louise's murder, after all, in a way."

His face was very near mine, and I could feel my breath going shallow. This was not the face of a boy; the features had hardened; the cheekbones showed under the rounded cheeks, the mouth had thinned down to anger; the blue eyes were narrowed against me.

"Sydney," he said, "I like you. I'm very attracted to you, as it happens, but I'm not going to let you jeopardize my career or my life. Can you imagine what the police could do with this? I was the last person to see Louise alive. Perhaps even now they're not too satisfied with my alibi. I know they've tried very hard to find some loophole in my timetable for that night. If they were to link me with the word 'Communism,' I'd be immediately suspect again. The word is anathema in this country. I could swear that it was an act of college-boy rebellion, but they'd never quite believe me."

I had to agree with him in part. "But that wouldn't give you a motive for murdering Louise. After all, you're being blackmailed, too. You're a victim."

He said scornfully, "If they're looking for a scapegoat, they'll forget reason."

I said slowly, "Or they could suspect you of being one of the blackmailers, I suppose. Heather Smith could have gathered the material about you as a form of insurance, in case you decided to take over the business."

He looked astounded for a moment; then an expression of amusement crossed his face, and he said, "It's perfectly possible, isn't it? I might be a consummate actor, I suppose."

"Yes, you could."

"Well," he said, "I can only give you my word that I'm not an extortionist, and ask you once again to give me those papers."

There was a long silence, stubborn on my part, increasingly angry, I thought, on his.

Then I capitulated. "Why not?" I said. "It's your secret, after all. You've a right to tell or not, as you see fit. Wait. I'll be back in a moment."

I went into the house, carefully locking the back door after me. I knew it was foolish. Either I must trust Felix completely, or not trust him at all. Yet I didn't want him to follow me into the house and see the secret room.

When I took the typed page of facts out to him, he thanked me quietly. Then he said, "I must be going. I was wondering—are you free for dinner tonight, Sydney? It might do both of us good to go out and forget our problems."

"Oh, I'm sorry, Felix," I said, and I was, rather. "I already have a dinner date for tonight. Perhaps another time."

He looked faintly surprised, and I knew that he was re-membering the way I had shied away from double dates with him and Louise.

"Are you planning to go to the recital at Hoffman Hall Friday night?" he asked.

"I think I should," I said. "Cecily is giving a piano recital, and I know the other performers slightly from seeing them around the school."

"Then why not have dinner with me on Friday and go to the recital after that?"

"I'd like that."

We made arrangements to meet at school on Friday, and then Felix went on his way. I picked up the tea things and went into the house, followed closely by Thomas, who seldom let me out of his sight when I was at home.

With the falling sun, the Indian-summer day had taken on a chill, and I shivered a little. Louise's death had drawn me, in spite of myself, out of my little cocoon, and I wasn't sure I liked it. I felt like a sponge, soaking up the troubles of the people around me. Something terrifying lay just around the corner, but I hadn't the faintest notion of what it was, nor from which direction it was coming.

## 17

*Fear in a handful of dust.*
—T. S. Eliot

Getting ready for my dinner engagement, I began to feel a little excited. It had been so long since I'd accepted a date with a man. Or was this a date? Perhaps Domenic Lawrence merely wanted to question me subtly. Perhaps he was as suspicious of me as I was of him. Perhaps, perhaps, perhaps. I was weary of the whole complicated mess, and once again I toyed with the idea of taking some of the money Louise had left me and going off to Europe. I'd always longed to visit the land in which I had my roots: Scotland and Skye and the Outer Hebrides. The memory of the peaceful night on Moon Island was so appealing that I pictured myself happily on some similar tiny island in the Hebrides, alone except for a handful of villagers who would neither know nor care who I was. Blue sky, gray rocks, blue sea: it sounded like a wonderful place to wash away the soiled memories.

Then I shook myself. My father had been a man gentle with others and stern with himself. He would have said, "There's no place to run, if you're trying to hide from yourself."

And of course it was true. Sooner or later I would have to face myself and my grief and my disillusionment about Jed. Sooner or later, I must come to terms with life, make myself pick up the pieces, start over again. I had taken back my maiden name, run away from California, and life was no simpler than before. I had merely exchanged one set of problems for another.

Besides, I reminded myself practically, wills took a long

time to probate; I would not receive that money quickly. And then I was ashamed, because I could think of the advantages of having ten thousand dollars, forgetting every now and again the reason for my acquisition: the death of a friend.

Defiantly, I ran myself a luxurious bath, replete with bubble beads and fine French-milled soap which had been a gift from Louise. I had just started to climb into the old-fashioned tub with the four lions' feet, when the telephone rang.

"Damn!" I said, but pulled on a robe and ran down to answer.

I caught it on the fifth ring.

"Sydney!" It was the same breathy voice, and I shivered.

Why was it so terrifying, this sexless fragment of a voice? It could not harm me. We were separated, if not by miles, then certainly by some distance, however minute. He wasn't in the house; he was at the other end of the telephone line.

I summoned up strength. "What do you want?" I asked, my voice as cold and detached as though someone were calling the wrong number.

The whisperer laughed. It was completely chilling, a laugh sized down to a whisper, but I would not give in to fear.

"What is it you want?" I asked again. "Coward! Why can't you speak out?"

Again the soundless, whispered laugh. "I know you have some papers that don't belong to you, Sydney. Put them— all of them—in a neat package and put it in a locker at Eastway Shopping Mall. Lock the door and put the locker key under the seat of the outdoor telephone booth in front of the branch post office at Eastway."

I was shaking violently. The whispered instructions were unspeakably frightening. The silver thread of voice was full of command, as though its owner were absolutely certain that I would not dare to disobey.

"Fasten the key securely to the bottom of the seat with Scotch tape, so it won't fall off and be found by someone else. Do it by two o'clock tomorrow afternoon. And Sydney—"

I said nothing.

"Don't wait around hoping to find out who I am. Remember—I know you, but you don't know me."

I said boldly, "I don't know what you're talking about. I have no papers."

The thread of voice vibrated with amusement. "Oh, I think you found something in Toronto when you were there. I might have killed you then, Sydney, if that bungling idiot of a woman hadn't come rushing out."

"Yes, I know," I said angrily, "but I won't make it so easy for you again." I waited for an answer, but when none came, I said, "I have nothing you could possibly want," and hung up the phone.

In another moment the instrument rang again angrily, but I sat there and let it go on ringing, while I watched the leaf shadows on the wall. There was a big poplar outside the sitting-room window, and the sun caught up the delicate tracery of branches and leaves and projected them onto the wall in a delicate fawn-colored silhouette.

Finally the shattering, persistent noise stopped, and I got to my feet lamely, like an old woman. I was held in a vise of fear, so that it was an effort to move, first to the front door, then to the back, to check the locks.

They were perfectly secure, of course; Miss Grimes's heavy, old-fashioned doors had big brass locks and keys roughly the size of jail keys; and in addition, the back door had a bolt. I shook the doors to make doubly certain they were locked, then went back upstairs to my cooling tub.

The luxurious froth had dwindled down to a thin scattering of rainbow-hued bubbles floating on the bath water. I climbed in, but it was a full five minutes before I felt really warm again.

I had plenty of time; Domenic had said seven. I went and lay on my bed, pulling the flowered coverlet over me to prevent the chill from returning.

If Heather Smith was the blackmailer, it seemed more and more likely that she had an accomplice. The whisperer on the telephone had sounded like a man, and the ruthless attempt to run me down in the motel parking lot—surely that was a man's deed?

Obviously, though, if her accomplice existed, he didn't know where she had hidden her little cache of information. Because, despite what he had said, I thought he wasn't sure that I had found anything in Toronto. It seemed to me that he was anxious to get me off the trail, to force me to leave Newton and go home to California. That way he'd be safe enough, conducting his nasty little business.

Beginning to dress, more carefully than I liked to admit to myself, I felt surprisingly cheerful. If my enemy didn't know for certain that I had the blackmail files, then perhaps I was reasonably safe for the time being—unless Heather should return suddenly to her grandmother's house and find the envelope gone.

And for the moment, I didn't really care. I was going to pretty myself up and go out with a man undeniably attractive and mysterious. For all I knew, he might be my sinister caller, yet my mind shrank away from this possibility. Forthright, even rude, he might be; icily cold on occasion, he most certainly was; but sly, crafty, reptilian, as the voice on the telephone, Domenic Lawrence was not.

I admired myself in the big looking glass which topped the old-fashioned mahogany dresser. The dress was right: coral silk, sleeveless, not restful like the blues and grays I usually wore. I had loosed my yellow hair tonight, so that it fell softly about my shoulders, instead of being neatly disciplined by a chignon. I refused to reach for the symbolism any good psychologist would have found in that fact. I knew the soft hair style was becoming, that it made me look younger and gentler and more vulnerable, and I didn't care.

"I suppose you wouldn't take kindly to a suggestion of dinner at my apartment?" Domenic said when he arrived. "It's perfectly all right if you'd rather go to a restaurant, but I thought I'd pick up a box of Louise's books and records.

She left them with me when she moved, and I thought you might give them to some of her friends as keepsakes."

"Of course," I said. The idea that Domenic Lawrence might be inviting me to his flat in order to have his way with me was eminently laughable. It was perfectly obvious that I was little more than a sounding board for his bitterness and grief over Louise.

He helped me into his car. "I'd hoped you might agree," he said, "so I bought a couple of steaks and some French bread and wine."

While the big car slid along the city streets, we carried on a pleasant, impersonal conversation. He was very knowledgeable about books and music, very quick and impatient in his likes and dislikes. I found myself enjoying our conversation, enjoying him, actually, and I had a little twinge of regret because we weren't, either of us, free of memories, free of old bitterness, old regrets.

He lived in one of the new luxury apartment houses, but his furniture was anachronistic, solid and good. He gave me a drink and a magazine, refusing to let me go into the kitchen to help. "If there's one thing I know how to do, it's cook a steak." He sounded almost lighthearted, and I looked at him in surprise. I would never have expected my presence to cheer him so.

Finally he relented enough to let me make the salad, and we worked along companionably until dinner was ready. It made me feel faintly melancholy, working thus in a kitchen with a man at my side. In those first months with Jed, before I'd known the truth about him, we had been happy; sometimes he would come into my tiny kitchenette, put his arms around me from behind, and nuzzle my hair. "It smells wonderful," he'd say. "You and the dinner. Let me help, let me mix my masterful salad dressing." Well, that was over and done, and this moment was good, too.

"Bring the salad and bread," Domenic ordered, bearing our plates of inch-thick steak. "Now is the moment to test my cooking."

I liked the decor, or lack of it, a pleasant mixture of old

and new. The dining table was a mahogany gate-leg, set before the crackling fire.

"My mother's," he said, when I admired it. "You may not believe it, but I have a sentimental attachment to things—and to people."

"I believe it," I said, after a moment, as I touched the old cranberry water glasses, gleaming in the firelight. "You've never married?" The words slipped out, unmeant.

For once the cold mask failed to slip over his face. "I was married briefly, when I was in law school. It was a mistake and ended in annulment. It didn't leave any deep scars, but I suppose it made me wary."

"Until you met Louise." I said it calmly. It was like biting on a sore tooth.

He nodded. "I think so. She was different, original, and exciting in her outlook. She had a mind like a steel trap, and I liked that."

Then he asked keenly, "And you?" I had an eerie feeling he was reading my mind.

Well, why not? I thought. Worse things have happened to people. Why should I hide? At least the voice on the telephone would be robbed of a weapon against me, if I forced myself to tell my secret to the people I'd grown fond of.

"I was married, also briefly," I said. "Jed, my husband, came from an affluent middle-class family. He'd dropped out of college, he was part of a surfing crowd. I met him at a party at Big Sur. To me he was part of it all, the rocks and the sea and the music and the artists and writers at the party. We were married within a month."

I sipped the brandy and tried not to remember the first happy days. "Jed was charming and intelligent, but weak, I suppose. He worked at a series of odd jobs, in the short time we were married, but he never stuck to anything. We kept moving around."

Domenic's brown eyes were fixed on my face, but he didn't interrupt.

"I'll never know what motivated Jed. He'd had everything he'd wanted, all his life. His parents would happily have paid for his education; his father would have given him a job. Instead, when things got tight, he and some friends robbed a gas station. The attendant was shot. He lived, but apparently Jed didn't realize it, because he ran when the police captured him." I deliberately made my voice emotionless. "He was shot, and died in my arms."

I felt the strong, warm hand cover my two hands, and inexplicably, without warning, the hot tears began belting down my cheeks.

"It's all right," he said gently. "Maybe we should all cry more."

The unexpected kindness nearly undid me, and I sat without talking for some time. Then, purely on impulse, purely illogically, since I could not be certain of his innocence, I began to tell him about Heather Smith and the blackmail letters and the money Louise had been sending to Heather.

His lips thinned with anger. "Damned little fool!" he said. "Why didn't she come to me for advice? I'd have told her not to pay. There are ways of dealing with blackmailers."

I gave him a skeptical look. "I think she tried dealing with them on her own. I think that's why she was killed—because she refused to pay."

"I take it you think there's more than one person involved. Do you think this Heather Smith is the payee, or the brains behind the thing, or what?"

I shuddered. "I think it must have been a man who killed Louise, but the money was addressed to Heather Smith, who very conveniently left Toronto on a trip to Europe. Actually, I think she may be here in Newton." I looked at him fairly. "You've heard that name, haven't you? You reacted to it."

He said reluctantly, "Yes. Once Louise spilled the contents of her purse, and I helped to pick them up. There was a long white envelope addressed to Heather Smith in Toronto. I remember that Louise became very angry when I picked it up—out of all proportion to the incident. Then she apologized. But it was a very uncomfortable little scene."

He looked at me sharply. "Have you informed the police of all this?"

"I can't," I said. "It would involve other people, and I have no right to do that without their permission."

"You're being very foolish, you know. If anyone has an inkling that you know something about this blackmail scheme, you might very easily be the next victim."

I shrugged. "If you're born to be hanged, you'll never be drowned."

He gave me an exasperated look. "It's all very well to believe in kismet, but there's no sense in being foolhardy. The police would be discreet, I assure you. And it might help them considerably, if they had some idea of a motive for Louise's death. As it is, they'll probably write it off as an unsolved killing, because it does look as though it might have been the work of a sniper."

I shook my head stubbornly. "No." I had had enough of police to last me a lifetime. And I was amazed to realize that I didn't really care much whether they caught Louise's murderer or not, just so long as he didn't kill anyone else.

"Well," said Domenic, "it's up to you, of course."

We talked about impersonal things after that, until finally I told him I must go, and he went to get Louise's books and records from a storage closet.

While he was gone, I gazed about, trying to fit the man and the surroundings together. On a leather-topped lamp table at my elbow, there was a volume of T. S. Eliot, face down and open, as though someone had been reading it and left it there.

I picked it up. It was open at "The Waste Land" and I read a few lines:

And I will show you something different from either
Your shadow at morning striding behind you
Or your shadow at evening rising to meet you;
I will show you fear in a handful of dust.

I turned to the flyleaf, and two words leapt out at me: "Louise Albright." Then, when I looked around me, the evidence of her vanished presence was everywhere: a blurred snapshot in a silver frame, a bundle of sheet music on a dusty wooden bench, a golden hair caught in the fabric of the big wing chair by the fireplace.

I was seized by an emotion I had thought long dead, a sick, painful twisting of the vitals which I could only call jealousy. I skirted around a good and logical reason for this feeling. Was I jealous of a dead woman?

Domenic, carrying a large cardboard carton, came back into the room, and I looked at him with new eyes. "Elegant" was still the word which first came to mind in describing him, but his tanned, square face looked drawn, I saw, as though he had been sleeping badly.

"Here they are," he said. "This one is marked 'Books,' and there's another marked 'Records.' Keep what you like and pass the others along to anyone you think might care to have them."

"All right," I said, adding curiously: "How is it that you don't know Louise's other friends really well?"

He paused in the doorway. "Oh, I've met most of them, I suppose. But I think she was inclined to keep her life in compartments, so to speak. I was in a different compartment from her friends at Hoffman."

You were the one she loved, I thought. That's why she never talked about you. You meant too much to her. I felt Louise's mind opening up before me, so that I could see inside for just a split second, and then it closed again. But I knew that I was right. In her own odd, undemonstrative way, Louise had loved Domenic Lawrence. They had loved each other.

"I'm afraid I must go home now," I said, suddenly weary of everything and everyone.

"I'll take you home, then." No polite protests, no urging to have another drink, no grand seduction scene. I could have laughed aloud, except that it didn't seem entirely funny. It made me feel drab and worn and used up, somehow.

In the big Lincoln, I could feel him looking at me from

time to time, as though trying to assess my mood. Finally he said, "Are you going to the recital at Hoffman Hall on Friday?"

I nodded.

"Well, then, why not have dinner with me downtown and let me take you to the recital afterward?" He turned toward me for a moment, to give me an unexpected, charming smile. "After what you've told me tonight, I feel that we have a great deal in common, don't you? Perhaps we can console each other."

I hated to say no; I found myself wanting to see him again. The process was like the slow cracking of ice on a frozen pond at winter's end; it was uncertain and uncomfortable, but it was the due process of nature. I wanted to go out with him.

But I had to say, "I'm sorry. I would have enjoyed it. But Felix Reichmann stopped by today, and suggested the same thing. So I'm afraid I'm committed."

With Domenic, the ice froze over again very quickly, leaving no trace of melting. "Oh, I see," he said. "I hadn't realized you felt obliged to comfort all the men Louise left behind her."

I couldn't imagine why I had thought for a moment that I could warm to this man, could find him attractive. I hated the sneer which twisted his firm, disciplined mouth, and I found myself in such a rage with him that I could say nothing. When he pulled up at 1 Greenwood Place, I leaped out of the car before he could move, flung an ungracious thank-you in his direction, and fled into the house, my sanctuary.

Why did I feel lonely, once I was inside my safe little house? Why should I miss the warm, vital presence of the man with whom I was so angry? I wanted to run to the door and call him back, but I could hear the motor roar as the Lincoln tore down the quiet little cul-de-sac. He had gone, and he was coldly annoyed with me, in any case. I had no talent left for dealing with people, especially with men.

I switched on lights and turned on music defiantly, but the little house did not respond tonight. It was cold and almost hostile to me. The October dampness seemed to seep in through the cracks, and I was seized by an unnamed devil.

With relief, I fell upon the thought of Thomas, with his noble head, his adoring gaze, his insouciant air. By now he would be heartily tired of the dish of crunchy kernels of dry cat food which I left for him in the basement each morning. He would be craving a tin of kidney and gravy, or a bit of ground beef. Thomas ate with all the gusto of a stevedore, sucking up cat or dog food, meat, bread, doughnuts, and olives with the joy of one who has a perfect digestion.

I switched on the cellar light and called down the stairs, but there was no answering cry, which meant that he had gone out the broken cellar window and would be waiting on the back steps.

When I opened the back door, I could hear Thomas crying plaintively, far off in the distance.

"Come on, Tom," I called.

The dark garden loomed up menacingly, and I shivered a little, as though something more than darkness waited out there. On the concrete walk, just outside the dark-green latticework which sheltered part of the back porch, three tall metal trash cans stood neatly side by side, their galvanized metal shining brightly in the light from the kitchen. Beyond them, I could see nothing but blackness.

I heard Thomas cry out again, in pain or fright, and I called him, this time more frantically. He answered me. There is no mistaking the urgency in a cat's voice when he is frightened or hurt, and I started to run out into the lonely dark garden, to rescue him from his predicament.

Something stopped me. I was alarmed about the poor, terrified cat, but suddenly something said: Wait, don't go out into the darkness all alone.

Whirling about, I ran back into the kitchen and searched out a flashlight in one of the drawers. Thomas' anguished cry rang out again, and I hurtled out the back door to save him.

I shone my light on the small, enclosed garden, on the crumbling stone wall with glossy ivy climbing it. The shaft of light pointed up the few hardy autumn flowers still remaining and the swath of green grass turned black by the flashlight's beam. I remember thinking that it all looked lonely and sinister somehow, this place which I had so loved on golden summer days and crimson autumn afternoons. Then I heard Thomas' frightened cry again, and I went toward the little garden door which opened onto a small, brick-paved alley. With my hand already on the bolt, I stopped. As surely as though I saw him, I could feel the presence on the other side of the little green door.

I heard Thomas' plaintive mew again, then the merest breath of a laugh, so faint that I might have thought I imagined it, had Thomas not come swarming over the wall, his silken fur the color of flame, his eyes shining with terror. I wanted to jerk open the door in the wall and look into the alley, but I dared not. Instead I ran, Thomas in my arms, back to the safety and shelter of 1 Greenwood Place.

I bolted the door; then I set Thomas on the counter and looked him over carefully. He was unhurt, but someone had frightened him badly. It was written in the way he sprang to my shoulders and crouched there, his big head hidden in my hair, his claws digging a little uncomfortably into the soft skin of my shoulder.

I opened Miss Grimes's shiny white refrigerator and took out a little saucer of chopped liver and set it on the counter. He took one glorious sniff, then leaped lightly, for all his bulk, onto the counter and began to eat, his fears forgotten in the satisfying aftermath of unlimited liver.

I lacked the cat's power of quick recovery. I found that I was shaking as though I had been in grave physical danger. I had to keep reassuring myself that such was not the case. Yet I went around pulling all the shades, drawing the heavy red-velvet draperies in the sitting room, testing the doors to make sure they were locked.

Then I put the kettle on to boil for tea and sat down weakly at the kitchen table. Thomas looked up from his dinner, gave me a brief, inquiring "Meow?" and went back to work.

I made the tea and carried it on a tray into the sitting

room. For some reason, I couldn't bear the thought of going to bed. It seemed to me that, while I lay in my bed, tense, not sleeping, the possessor of the Voice might break in somehow, wander through the downstairs rooms, seeking the material which he suspected me of having, the material which apparently provided him with a very comfortable livelihood.

I switched on the television set, to keep from thinking, but the insidious little thoughts kept creeping through. I was becoming more and more convinced that my pursuer had meant only to frighten me tonight, rather than cause me any physical harm. He had taunted me, jeered at me, terrified my poor cat, in malice. I felt sure that his deeper purpose was to frighten me into giving up the dossiers I had found in Toronto. Then he wanted me to leave Newton and forget what I'd learned about Heather Smith.

It all made sense. I held evidence which could condemn the blackmailer, and very possibly the murderer, if the police should find him. In addition, I had the equivalent of a small fortune hidden away in the secret room, although he couldn't be sure of that.

If you were smart, Sydney Webster, I thought, you'd do what he wants you to do. Of course, I couldn't return the envelopes to him, but I could burn them. And I could go back to California and be out of harm's way. It was the sensible thing to do, but I was no longer very sensible. I was angry.

## 18

*I cried for madder music and for stronger wine.*
        —ERNEST DOWSON

The funereal hush had lingered over the Hoffman Conservatory of Music for days, but on the morning of the recital, the atmosphere lightened perceptibly. As I worked in my little office, I could hear the scraping of violin bows against the strings, the soft testing of notes on flutes and horns.

Cecily came in and perched on a corner of the desk, filling the air with smoke, as always. She feigned indifference to the concert, but I sensed that she was apprehensive and terribly keyed up under her cool exterior.

"I really do hope I make it," she confessed finally, grinding out her third cigarette in my clean ashtray. "Then I'll get my degree and can shake the dust of Newton off my shoes in the spring. I think I'll go to New York. There's no percentage in any permanent arrangement for Lucien and me, anyway, although he's a very exciting man. But I want to get Tina out of here, somewhere safe."

I had stopped typing politely, and now I said, "What did you do about the last demand for money?"

She raised a cynical eyebrow. "Paid it. What else? I can't afford to take chances." She got up. "Well. You're coming tonight, aren't you?"

"Wouldn't miss it," I assured her. "You'll be great, never fear."

When she opened the door, I saw Paul Fleming and Barbara Carmichael walking hand in hand down the corridor. They saw me, and Barbara gave me a friendly smile and drew Paul into my office.

"Do you have tickets for tonight?" she asked. "I'd love to have you come and hear me. I'm doing a violin solo, you know."

I smiled at her. She was pretty as an ad for French bath soap. "Yes, I know," I said. "I sent the program to the printer, and I saw your name. Are you nervous?"

"Gibbering with fear."

Paul Fleming smiled down at her. "You're going to be wonderful, and you know it."

Barbara smiled at him, pride and affection making her face even prettier. "He plans to be a conductor, you know, so I have to please his critical ear."

He grinned. "Yes. My standards are of the highest, in musicians and wives." Then, with the polite, serious deference which made me feel a thousand years older than they, he added, "Do you have tickets, Miss Webster? We have two extras, if you need them. I imagine you could stand a little recreation, after what you've been through."

"Thank you." I was touched by their solicitude. "I'm going with Felix Reichmann, and I know he has tickets."

They went off together, and I resumed my typing, feeling faintly cheered and warmed by the thought that I was making friends at last, that there were people concerned, if only perfunctorily, with my well-being.

At the end of the day I closed my typewriter, tidied up my desk, and went into the first-floor ladies' room to freshen my makeup and change into a silky black-velvet dress which had been my one extravagance that fall. I pinned on a chignon and piled my blond hair high around it, and when I'd finished, I was pleased, not only because I looked particularly festive, but because there was color in my cheeks and anticipation in my eyes. I had begun to treasure each sign of returning life, as though it were an unexpected, undeserved gift.

Felix came into my little office at six, and I was rather flattered by the look of pleasure on his face. "You look beautiful, Sydney!" he said. "I don't know why I hadn't realized it before. I think it's because I've never seen you so animated, so lighted up."

We went to dinner at a little French restaurant with red-and-white-striped wallpaper and Victorian decor and sat long over the duck à l'orange and the white wine and the petits fours. A little pedantic in manner, Felix Reichmann was still an interesting conversationalist, full of fascinating little anecdotes about famous personalities in the music world.

Once again, of course, we went over the mystery of Louise's death, the identity of the blackmailer, but reached no conclusion. Yet it was like a nagging tooth that one's tongue kept returning to involuntarily.

Finally we left the restaurant, got into Felix' little Volkswagen, and drove back to Hoffman Hall, which was in the Hoffman Conservatory complex. It was a small, luxurious theater, acoustically perfect for recitals and for performances by the Hoffman Philarmonic Orchestra.

"Do you realize Louise would probably be performing tonight?" Felix asked, as we settled into our seats in the rapidly filling theater.

"Was she good?" I asked curiously. "I heard her once or twice at the Ferris Wheel, but I couldn't really judge from that, of course."

"She was competent. I'm sure she had no idea of becoming a professional performer, but she would have been a good teacher, if . . ."

If she had lived.

The seats were filling rapidly now. Everywhere there were students in their motley garments; bearded boys in turtlenecks and leather jackets and tight jeans and corduroys; girls with long, straight hair, girls with short curly hair, and a fair smattering of people of all ages dressed in their theatergoing best.

It was a musical crowd, and one I found eternally fascinating. I'd forgotten how much I had loved the concerts with Mother and Daddy, in the old days; the scrape of the fiddles as they tuned up, the rustle of the programs and the murmur of voices, the rich velvet of the curtains, the lowering of the lights, the wonderful, mystical magic as the orchestra began the overture. I settled back contentedly.

First on the program was Diana Walters, a lovely Titian-haired girl with a glorious mezzo-soprano voice. After that came Barbara Carmichael, playing the violin well but not brilliantly, and looking so pretty and well-cared-for that one knew instinctively that the smallness of her talent would make no great difference to her life.

"Cecily is next," Felix whispered.

She looked tiny before the grand piano, but there was such power, such majesty in her performance, that I found my antagonism toward her melting away, for the moment, at least. I could grant her a certain amount of license, simply because she was capable of giving great beauty to the world.

"Let's go backstage for a minute and congratulate Cecily," I said to Felix when the performance was over.

There were dozens of friends and relatives milling about the rehearsal-room-greenroom in the rear of the little theater. I saw Domenic there. He went up to shake Cecily's hand and say something to her, leaning over her from his great height. He was so tall that he stood out above the crowd of well-wishers. When he caught my eye, I nodded and smiled at him, but there was no answering smile. He nodded soberly and went out of the room.

Cecily, her brown hair long and straight as a little girl's tonight, was radiant in a costly white chiffon evening dress which must have cost her ex-husband a pretty penny, I thought.

"Cecily, you were wonderful," I said. "I truly didn't realize how gifted you are. Congratulations!"

She gave me one of those theatrical hugs which all performers seem to exchange, but there was a certain amount of warmth there, all the same, and I saw a momentary mist in her perfectly made-up eyes.

"Thanks, Sydney," she said, "I'm terribly glad you came."

We talked to her for a few minutes, then went to congratulate Barbara Carmichael, who was looking exceedingly pretty, with a wild-rose flush on her cheeks.

"I'm so glad you came," she said, glowing at our praise. "Paul is here somewhere. Did you see him?"

As we walked away, I heard her thanking a distinguished-looking couple for their compliments, and not for the first time, I felt a pang of envy for this girl, so lovely to look at, talented and rich, yet so sweet and modest. Her life lay open before her, like a smooth and beautiful road, and I wondered why hers had been so ordained, while Irene's path and Louise's and mine were so muddled and difficult.

The performers and their friends and relatives were milling around the makeshift greenroom. Someone was passing around a big pitcher of martinis, lifting it high over our heads. It was beaded with moisture, and I began to thirst for something cold, here in the scent-laden air of the crowded room.

"Could we possibly latch onto some of that beverage?" I asked Felix, and he went off amiably to find some paper cups.

While I waited, pressed against the cool, dun-painted wall, I looked at the other people, some familiar, most of them not. Except perhaps for relatives of the performers, this was a crowd of music lovers, a curiously charming, lively group, I thought, different in an intangible way from a group of art lovers or writers or actors. I was intrigued by the idea that each coterie of creative artists, and members of one profession or another, were part of a little world of their own, self-contained and self-sufficient. There could be an occasional overlapping, of course, but for all practical purposes, there was automatic segregation of the arts and professions.

I saw Harry Livermore, the local music critic, talking to Barbara Carmichael and Cecily. This meant a good review for them in tomorrow morning's paper. If he had disliked their performances, he would have been the first one out of Hoffman Hall, and completely conspicuous by virtue of his smallness, his glittering black eyes behind big, horn-rimmed glasses, and his spadelike Vandyke beard. I felt quite pleased for all of the performers, and particularly for Cecily, toward whom I felt benevolent tonight.

Then I heard a little gabble of voices, and saw Phil Valenti lift Irene onto the battered grand piano. It was only then that I realized he was two inches shorter than she.

"Everyone—listen to me!" Irene said. She wore a jet-black dress and dangly loops of jet beads, and I thought she looked like an old-time torch singer. I half-expected a throaty, sexy song to come out of those perfect lips. She waved a champagne glass filled with sparkling burgundy and said, "I have an announcement. Phil and I are going to have a baby!"

Everyone made some suitable comment, and there was some light applause. Then I heard Cecily drawl, "High time. I should think yours is the love affair of the century. It should be perpetuated."

I saw Irene turn white, and I knew that the word "affair" had hit home, whether Cecily had meant anything by it or not. I wanted to hit her, as I often found myself wanting to hit Cecily. One could imagine her as a lady-in-waiting, in some long-ago court, whispering malicious bits of court gossip into the queen's ear, stirring up all sorts of trouble for the others in the palace. If it hadn't been for her fierce love for her daughter and her undeniable musical gift, I could quite cheerfully have hated Cecily.

Irene turned her head slowly and mysteriously, and I could see that she was the queen after all, a tragic and noble queen, who would listen to no backbiting from one of her subjects.

"Yes," she said, her magnificent eyes sweeping Cecily's face, "if you are truly in love, a child is the ultimate result, it seems to me."

I saw Lucien's dark, oblique look at Cecily, and I realized that his passion for her was an all-encompassing thing. I'd never been aware of any real intensity on his part before. Now I saw that his feeling for her was devastating, while Cecily's, I knew, was a passion of the moment. I wondered sadly what would happen to him when Cecily received her master's degree and went off to New York to work. Lucien's faith in himself was all too frail as it was; I hated to think of him hurt and disillusioned, which he inevitably would be.

Watching them all, feeling like a skeleton at the feast, I found myself thinking of something else, something vaguely disturbing. And then I knew what it was.

At least one of the blackmailers could very easily be here among the music lovers. It was someone who knew well, if not intimately, the people at Hoffman Conservatory. Why shouldn't he be a part of this murmuring, enthusiastic crowd? And if he were, then Irene had just given him another weapon in their one-sided battle.

It seemed to me then that I could feel it in the air, the little wind of hate, the sense of evil for evil's sake, which I had felt in the funeral home, just before I found that first note.

"Times like this, I wish I'd had the ability to be a performer, rather than a teacher," Felix said, coming back with our drinks. "It's exciting, isn't it?"

"Very exciting."

"And wonderful news for Phil and Irene."

"Wonderful." I glanced over at the two at the piano. Irene was radiant, as though she'd been given a splendid, unique gift. Despite her problems, I found myself envying her. To love single-mindedly was no little thing.

"I think I'd better go, Felix. Would you mind walking me to my car?" I had left the MG in the school parking lot that morning.

"If you won't go somewhere for another drink?"

"No, thank you," I said. "I really am tired." And I was, my face stiff with smiling.

We went into the crowded cloakroom where we had hung our coats, and he took my plain black coat off the hanger and stood holding it, smiling down at me.

He was so completely charming, this Felix, a far cry from Domenic Lawrence, with his long, cryptic silences, his terse comments, his indefinable air of standoffishness. By contrast, Felix was affable, gregarious, yet sensitive. He did everything so perfectly, making me feel like a woman, admired and cherished. When he held my coat for me, it was like a lover's caress. I knew that he must do this for every woman; it was his life fashion, as a much-in-demand bachelor-about-town. Still, it was undeniably flattering.

I smiled up at him, and he leaned closer to kiss the little hollow in my shoulder. His nice, almost boyish face was very close to mine, and I thought it exceptionally open and attractive. His mouth was rather small and vulnerable, and his brown hair was as wavy as a small boy's when he comes from the swimming pool. There was something like Jed about him, not so much in actual features, but in the curving little smile, the thick, dark lashes.

I closed my own eyes against the pain, and he said, "What is it? What's wrong?"

I shook my head and gave him a stiff, artificial little smile. "It's nothing."

How could I tell him that I had realized nothing is necessarily what it seems? Jed had been, on the surface, a high-spirited, open young man, yet he had robbed, without a qualm of conscience. For all his seeming guilelessness, Felix had something to hide. At one time he had been a card-carrying Communist, even if he was one no longer. So his almost innocent, open, very good-looking face might conceal any amount of evil, after all? How could I possibly tell? My judgment was worthless.

"Where have you gone, Sydney?" he asked gently. "It's no good kissing someone who isn't even here."

"I was thinking how little I know you."

He looked surprised. "How well do you have to know me?"

I realized I was walking into deep waters. If I questioned Felix Reichmann about his past, what was to prevent him from questioning me? Just thinking about it made my spine rigid with nerves. I wasn't ready to tell anyone else about Jed and the unhappy months behind me, not even Felix, who was gentle and uncritical.

"It wasn't the kiss," I said absently.

"What, then?" He was looking at me oddly. "What do you want to know about me—and why?"

I smiled gaily. 'Don't pay any attention to me, Felix. I'm neurotic. I'll conquer it one of these days. And I did have a lovely evening, thank you."

We left the small, perfect little theater, which had been planned so carefully by Alfred Hoffman himself. The others would stay, I knew, very late, but I felt restless and uneasy, anxious to get away from the smiling, cultured, well-dressed people who seemed to have no real problems.

Don't be smug, I admonished myself. Probably they're tied up in knots inside. Some of them may be Heather Smith's victims. Think of Lucien and Phil and Irene.

We stepped out of the side door of Hoffman Hall into the crowded parking area. Parking was free to concert-goers, and there was no attendant. It was dark and quiet, and I shivered, thinking of Louise walking purposefully, unafraid, through the tiny city park, never thinking of danger. But then, she had been a fearless person; it was completely in character. Or had she, after all, been walking with someone, someone who had pretended to walk away, then shot her and left her to die?

For all I knew, I thought wryly, Felix Reichmann had pulled that trigger, and could equally well put his hands about my throat and strangle me, here within a few yards of the milling crowds at Hoffman Hall. When he put his hand on my arm and helped me into my car, I felt a moment of swift revulsion.

Then he said, in his customary, rather soft, gentle tones, "Thank you for going with me, Sydney. Let's do it again soon," and I could have laughed at my fears.

I drove home quickly, thinking of an offended Thomas, relegated to dry cat food and his own company for the entire day and evening. He had his own means of ingress and egress—one glassless pane in a cellar window, with a piece of heavy burlap covering it—but he preferred human companionship to that of the neighborhood cats. I was becoming quite spinsterish in outlook, I thought ruefully.

When I went up the front steps, he got up from the porch railing, stretched, and greeted me by rubbing his great head against my face.

"Come on, Thomas," I said. "Hamburg."

He trotted into the house with me and began to sniff the air.

"Yes, Thomas," I said slowly, "someone has been here! Someone has been smoking in this room since I left."

The sense of menace was so great that I wanted to run out of the house to the MG and go back to the Hoffman Conservatory, back to lights and people and safety. Yet I knew this was unrealistic. During the hours of my absence, from early that morning, anyone could have entered the house and searched it.

For I was convinced that someone had been searching for something. The drawers of the desk were slightly askew, as though someone had pushed them back carelessly. I went and looked inside each drawer. None of the innocuous things was missing, so far as I could see.

I forced myself to go from room to room, turning on lights, investigating drawers and cupboards, anything which I thought might have been searched. Nothing was missing, yet someone had been there. Finally I went and tried the long, narrow windows which faced the front porch. The one on the right was unlatched, although I had thought it locked. I tried to decide when I might have done this awesomely careless deed; perhaps when I'd been cleaning, the day before, and had raised the windows to air the room, I had forgotten to lock this one, thus providing an easy means of entry for my enemy. Although my enemy, I felt sure, would have found another way into the house in my long absence. In my absence! It *had* to be someone connected with Hoffman, someone who knew I could be counted on to be gone all day and evening, on this particular day.

I made myself a cup of tea in the quiet kitchen and took it back into the sitting room, where I sat huddled before the gas log, too frightened to think very clearly. I toyed with the idea of calling the police, but I knew they'd think me little more than neurotic. Nothing had been stolen, nothing had been seriously disturbed; no policeman would ever believe that I could be absolutely certain that someone had been in my house. Only a woman would have felt the subtle difference in drawers and desk, the intolerable feeling of violation.

The thing which frightened me most was the sense of deliberate malice. Someone had been here; someone had searched for something he hoped or feared I had; and that someone had not troubled to hide the fact of his visit from me. Yet, as surely as though I could hear a malevolent chuckle in the silent room, I knew he was laughing at me. He knew that he had ruffled the surface of my home ever so faintly, so that no one would believe me—and yet he didn't care in the least if I knew.

I felt certain that my tormentor was looking for the dossiers, but I also knew that he had another motive for his persecution. The terrifying telephone calls, the careless searching of my home, the nasty terrorizing of Thomas— these were not so much acts of violence as they were deeds of malice and hostility.

On a sudden impulse, uncaring about the hour, I picked up the telephone and put in a call to Joe Burnham at the Sailer Place address. To my surprise, actually, he answered. Apparently he lived in a flat over the antique shop, because his voice, irritable with interrupted sleep, came over in a few seconds' time.

"Yes, this is Joe Burnham."

"Mr. Burnham, this is Sydney Webster. I talked to you about Heather Smith."

There was a long pause, then the cool, antagonistic, "Yes?"

"I plan to leave for Toronto first thing in the morning, and I'd very much like to see you while I'm there."

His tone was guarded now. "Why do you want to see me?"

"I think you know," I said levelly, "that it's about Heather Smith. It has become increasingly obvious to me, these past few days, that she is not the person you imagine her to be."

"That's for me to judge, isn't it?"

"Not," I said, "when she is mixed up in blackmail and murder."

There was a long pause. Then he said, "I don't believe you, but I can't prevent you from coming here, can I? I'll be at the shop all day tomorrow. My uncle is on a buying trip in Quebec. Come around if you feel you must."

"I must," I said, and hung up.

Before I could crawl into the haven of my bed, I must sort out things for the next day. I went into the kitchen and sifted through the envelope of human misery which I'd brought back with me from Moon Island: the motley collection of Newton citizens with their secrets, their mean little transgressions.

When they were all spread out on the kitchen table, I chose a half-dozen—enough to convince Joe Burnham, I thought, and put the rest of the material back into the bulging manila envelope.

Then I went into the sitting room and made certain the velvet draperies were tightly drawn before I turned on the lights. I could not rid myself of the feeling that my enemy lurked about, ready to peer into the tiniest chink in the curtains. It was a ghostly feeling, and I thought how comforting it would be to rent a little house in Sausalito or Carmel and drive off to work each day, unencumbered by fears of invasion of privacy or worse.

In the big desk, mixed in with Louise's odds and ends, the bills and advertisements we'd both accumulated, the stamps and pads and notepaper, was a tan envelope of snapshots I'd picked up at the drugstore on the afternoon of Louise's death. In the jumble of tragedy and fear and worry, I'd completely forgotten them, but now I had a reason for remembering. In that envelope were a dozen snapshots which I'd taken at the last party Louise had given at 1 Greenwood Place. They were Kodachrome prints, all quite clear, with the exception of one, which had come out a complete blur, as my pictures frequently seemed to do.

In the harsh yellow kitchen light, I studied the snaps. They filled me with sadness. That had been a happy Sunday, with tea and cocktails, and fifteen or twenty of Louise's friends milling about the little house. Even I had softened a little that day, joining in the chatter, serving drinks and hors d'oeuvres, and shedding, as Louise put it, my "ice-blue Madonna" look. The music had been wonderful. Phil had played his violin and Anne Hartwig had sung to Louise's guitar accompaniment. It had been a very satisfying party, and I had loaded up my small Kodak and snapped a whole roll of color prints. If only one of them would mean something to Joe Burnham!

## 19

*Portraiture is not photography.*
　　—SAMUEL SHELLABARGER

In the morning, I arose early, showered under the old-fashioned ring shower in Miss Grimes's small cavern of a bathroom, and went downstairs.

"Sorry," I said to Thomas, who waited impatiently at the foot of the stairs, "but it's the kitchen and kitty litter for you today, friend. I can't take a chance on having you kidnapped while I'm gone."

He leaped onto the kitchen table, to await his portion of coffee cream, his bits of toast and scrambled egg. I prepared and ate them hastily today, even though it was Saturday, offending Thomas deeply by offering him the crusts of toast instead of the nice buttery parts he favored. While I ate, I glanced at the headlines. There was nothing about Louise's death. The case had made headlines the first few days, then had gradually died down to nothing. The last article had called it "another unsolved local killing."

I opened a tin of cat tuna and put it in Thomas' dish, filled his water bowl, then checked the kitchen window and door. After that I double-checked all the downstairs windows. Let him try to find an unlatched window this time, I thought grimly. I would suffocate from stale air before I'd give him another chance to search my home.

Finally, with everything secured tightly and Thomas locked sulking in the house, I went and got the MG out of the garage and drove down the quiet little street into the heavy traffic of early morning.

Once I had left the city, I felt a certain lifting of the heart. I couldn't believe that my enemy watched me night and day, and I had no feeling that he was following me on this clear and brilliant morning.

I thought of Domenic Lawrence and wondered if I would ever see him again. My mind spun little daydreams about him all the way to Toronto, the sort of daydreams I'd thought done and ended forever for me. I thought of the look with which he regarded me, a look sometimes quizzical, sometimes downright hostile, and only occasionally gentle and understanding.

Silly, I admonished myself, you're very silly. What have you to offer a man like this, after Louise? He might, I thought dismally, be attracted to someone like Cecily, some-one cool and poised and uncaring, someone who was un-doubtedly going to make a name for herself in the musical world.

No, after the mystery of Louise's death was solved, if it ever were solved, after I'd decided what to do with the blackmail notes, then I thought I'd give up the little house on Greenwood Place—although my heart twisted at the thought—and perhaps, take that trip to Europe. After that, I could go back to California and find a job.

I looked out onto the neat rows of brick houses which dot the environs of Toronto, so many brick ones, as opposed to the wooden houses on the American side of the border. All these tidy little homes must have families, groups of people leading nice, normal lives. Or did life seem placid only to the onlooker?

I did not hurry. I felt no urgency today. Yet, just to be on the safe side, I'd decided not to stay at the Queen's Inn, should it prove necessary for me to stay the night. I did not plan to tempt fate again. I would go carefully, tread-ing gingerly, from now on until I was safely out of Newton.

I parked the MG in a ramp garage and went into a de-partment store to have lunch. I thought that I would rather not face Joe Burnham on an empty stomach.

Recklessly I went into the book department to browse around. Half an hour later, I was still there, dazed by the wealth of reading material. Finally I chose an armful of paperbacks, feeling pleasantly guilty at my extravagance. But then, I remembered somberly, I was an heiress of sorts. I could afford a few extra books, a bottle of fine wine, a good winter coat, thanks to Louise.

I walked through the aisles, with their counters already showing signs of Christmas promotion, toward the tea room at the back of the main floor. There, while I ate my baked halibut and drank the fragrant tea, I looked over my little treasure trove of books and had pleasant thoughts of reading in bed that night, as late as I wished, with no necessity for getting up in the morning.

I thought of my father's hurt if he could know that I hadn't been to church in many months. I would come back to it, I knew that now, but I wasn't quite ready yet.

Even while I enjoyed the tea and resisted the cigarette I was learning to do without, my mind kept worrying away at the thought of Joe Burnham. I wasn't anxious to encounter his obvious antagonism any sooner than I had to, but the day was wearing on.

On my way out of the store, I bought a silky orange scarf, the color of an autumn leaf, and a small flask of expensive perfume. Clutching my purchases to me, I went back to the parking ramp and drove off in my car. I had today bought things I didn't actually need, but wanted. I thought that rather a good sign. Wanting things means wanting to live.

Driving along the busy city streets, I wondered briefly about poor old Mrs. Hungerford, Heather's grandmother. Had she ever found out that the papers were missing from Heather's old trunk? I rather thought not. Poor old thing, she wouldn't know if the contents of her entire cellar were removed.

I found Sailer Place easily enough, remembering the little twists and turns I'd taken last time. It was as dingy as I'd remembered it, and as shabbily quaint. The cobblestone street was hilly and narrow, and the MG perched half on and half off the sidewalk.

I entered the little shop to the tinkle of the tiny bell. The place was dusty and crowded, the bits and pieces of many lives on exhibit here. I saw a Swiss music box of carved wood, a small ivory goat, and a black lace fan, amidst the brooches and cuckoo clocks and silver spoons, flung there with artless care. The carrousel horse with the big black eyes was still there, and I was foolishly happy that no one had claimed him. Perhaps I would buy him myself one day, to guard Miss Grimes's garden, and later to ride endlessly in a sunny garden by the sea, among the flaming California poppies.

Joe Burnham was coming toward me from the back of the store. He walked with that confident, almost swaggering gait I'd noticed before, and he was as sulky-looking as ever, square and sturdy, with a measure of scorn in the glance of his blue eyes.

"Hello," he said. "I see you made it."

He was restless, and beneath the hostility, I sensed some deeper feeling of anxiety and fear. There were lines around the stubborn mouth, and dark smudges beneath the bold eyes. Something was worrying Joe Burnham, something which hadn't been there when I'd talked to him before.

"Come and sit down," he said, and led the way through a swinging oak gate to a little office crammed with catalogs and small *objets d'art* and an old rolltop desk stuffed with dusty invoices. He gave me the old swivel chair and sat down himself on an antique rush-bottomed chair which plainly needed gluing.

"Well," he said, "what did you want to see me about this time? You've dug up some more dirt about Heather?"

His tone challenged me to dispute, but I recognized something else—fear, perhaps, surely doubts of some kind— and so I failed to answer in kind.

"Have you heard from Heather?" I asked.

He hesitated, and for a moment I thought he was going to lie, then he said, "No, I haven't heard from her, and I must admit that I'm worried. When she left, she warned me that she never wrote letters, but it's been so long now. Surely she would have written me a note if she had decided to prolong her stay. She's simply dropped from view." He scowled. "I've been worrying ever since your last visit. I wish you'd never come."

"I think Heather is in Newton," I said quietly. "In fact, I'm sure of it." I took the manila envelope and spilled its contents onto the desk: newspaper clippings, photographs, typewritten lists of names, and some coldly incisive case histories of human beings, people with pathetic little tragedies or indiscretions to hide. In a few brief paragraphs, each life was laid bare on paper.

"I won't tell you how I came by these, but I give you my word, this material belongs to Heather Smith. It's all about people who live in Newton. It's obvious she must live there, too, in order to have gathered up this muck."

He glanced at them cursorily, distastefully. Then he said, "I suppose you're right. Not that it matters any longer, but it seems as though Heather must be in Newton now, whether or not she went to Europe when she left here."

"The point is," I said, "who is she? She certainly isn't using her own name. And she has—she must have—an accomplice. A man. Because a man threatened me on the phone, more than once, and I feel sure it was a man who tried to kill me at the motel here. It was too ruthless, too brutal for a woman to have done. I firmly believe it was the same man who killed Louise."

The ancient chair squeaked under his weight. He looked at me directly out of his cool blue eyes, which now held pain in their depths. "I realize you'd like me to go to Newton and meet the people you know there, to see if I recognize Heather." His face hardened. "Well, I won't do it. She may not be the girl I thought she was, and I may not approve of the way she's earning her dollar, but I'm not going to betray her to the police." He stood up. "So if that's all, Miss Webster . . ."

I couldn't just walk out of there without finding out. I had to know if Heather was someone I had met. "Please," I said. "Won't you just look at these snapshots?"

I took out the pictures one by one. "This is Phil Valenti and Irene."

Phil was smiling, making love to the violin; and Irene was at the piano, her eyes making love to Phil. Her playing was competent but uninspired, and she was happiest when Phil allowed her the privilege of accompanying him. It was all there in the quickly snapped picture.

Joe Burnham shook his head. "I've never seen them before in my life."

"Tony Ferris wasn't at the party, but obviously *he* isn't Heather," I murmured, turning over the pictures. "Now, this is Cecily Andrews. And Lucien King."

He looked at Cecily's picture closely, then shook his head. "She's the right size and coloring, but she's not Heather."

I peered at the faces in the background of the next photograph. "Here's Felix Reichmann, and Cecily again, and some I've met casually."

I turned up one of Louise, her head thrown back, eyes turned in the direction of the piano. "I suppose the police would have liked this," I said slowly. "She didn't like to have her photograph taken, and there were no likenesses of her to put in the newspapers."

I shuddered. "Except for that horrible, gruesome one taken in the park." And the misty, unclear one in Domenic's apartment, I thought.

Joe Burnham picked up the print and looked at it. Then he looked again, more carefully, his face paling. He spread his fingers over the bright hair.

"That's Heather," he said. "She's changed the color of her hair; she was dark-haired when I knew her. But that's Heather."

## 20

*My smile falls heavily among the bric-a-brac.*
—T. S. Eliot

The bell tinkled to announce the arrival of a customer. As always, in drama, in tragedy, the mundane intruded: the arrival of the milkman in the middle of a domestic quarrel, the paper boy's knock when one's face is drowned in tears, the cheerful telephone call from a friend when the heart-breaking letter is barely read.

Joe Burnham got to his feet automatically and went out into the shop, and I heard his voice answering a customer, reasonably, politely, one supposed. While I waited, I stared at last year's calendar, curling and dusty, hanging on a nail, at a little heap of tangerine peels, at the pigeonholes in the old rolltop desk, at the empty coffee cup perched precariously on the edge of the wooden shelf. All these things would be preserved forever in my mind, along with the memory of Joe Burnham's stark words: "That's Heather."

For him, I reminded myself, the shock was infinitely worse. Heather as Louise meant Heather dead. The dark-haired girl who'd supposedly gone to Europe had turned up in Newton as a blond, murdered Louise.

I couldn't think of any words of comfort for him. I knew the tragedy of sudden death, and I knew equally well the incredible, smashing blow of trust betrayed. To find Heather dead was one thing; to know she had been a blackmailer, feeding on the transgressions of others, was a far greater wound.

When he came back into the cluttered office, the swagger was gone, and the look of truculence had been wiped from his face, perhaps forever. He looked like a boy bereft of all he'd held dear, and I wanted to comfort him.

"I'm sorry," I said. "I know you loved Heather."

He sat down heavily. "Yes. But I didn't love Louise, did I? So it stands to reason I only loved half of Heather, the half I thought I knew." He looked at me in puzzlement. "How could I have worked with her and loved her, yet have known so little about her?"

"I think," I said slowly, "the answer is quite simple. When she worked here, she was Heather. When she became Louise Albright, she put Heather Smith behind her."

He got to his feet in one swift movement. "We can't talk here. Let's go around the corner to the Royal Oak and have a drink. I'll put a sign on the door. Business has been slow this week, anyway."

After he had locked up the little shop, we went out into the fresh autumn air and walked down the hilly, cobbled street to the next corner. The Royal Oak was a neighborhood saloon, a small, two-story building, where a white-aproned bartender wiped the bar desultorily with a piece of cheesecloth, and three or four men were playing cards at one of the wooden tables.

The bartender eyed us and waved. "Hiya, Joe. What'llya-have?"

"Hi, Bernie." He looked at me. "What will you have to drink?"

"A glass of Burgundy, please."

He picked up my wine and his own Scotch and led the way to a booth at the back. "We can sit here forever, if we want."

There was a long, uncomfortable silence, while I tried to sort out something useful to say, and Joe Burnham watched the card players as though his life depended on the outcome of their game. Finally he looked directly at me.

"Tell me about Louise," he said. "I don't think I can let you go away until I've found out all about her."

When I tried to put it in words, I found there was, after all, very little I knew about Louise.

"We never questioned each other," I said, in dull surprise. "Now that I think of it, we were like two Orientals, exquisitely polite to each other, backing away from anything which might seem embarrassing."

His blue eyes were like a stormy sea today, muddied and inscrutable. "You must know something, anything which ties her to Heather." He put his head in his hands. "My God, I'm going out of my mind, trying to figure out *why*. Why and how."

I put a pitying hand on his. "I'm afraid there is no question as to the why. I think perhaps Louise had always been deprived of love, because her parents died when she was very young. And so she began to substitute things for love—and she had to have money to buy things."

"Yes. That's why, I should imagine. But where do Heather and Louise run side by side, and where do they coincide?"

I sipped the wine slowly. "Louise was highly intelligent. I think she carried out a very simple, straightforward plan. She became another person; she taught herself to write with her right hand instead of her left, she changed her image.

"I believe she must have been born Heather Smith, and when she was orphaned, she was sent to her relatives in Chicago. I'm absolutely certain Louise was telling me the truth when she said that her aunt and uncle had reared her, and that both were dead."

He nodded. "It makes sense, in a weird sort of way."

"I think if only I'd looked at the other things in that trunk at Mrs. Hungerford's, I might have found something with the name Heather Louise on it. I don't know whether her aunt adopted her legally, or whether she just took their name, but I feel certain she was called Albright when she lived in Chicago. After all, her school records would show that, so she could hardly have lied about it."

We sat in silence for a while, while I tried to think myself into the mind of Louise Albright. "I suppose she must have been at loose ends, after her aunt died—she said that her uncle had died about five years ago—and possibly she went to stay with Mrs. Hungerford for a bit, then found the job with your uncle."

He nodded. "I think you must be right. Heather never said anything about her background, only that she was completely on her own, except for an elderly relative on the island."

He stood up. "I'll get us another drink," he said somberly, and walked toward the bar. I heard the cheerful bartender chatting away, and felt certain Joe Burnham didn't hear a word. He came back slowly, bearing an overfull glass of deep-red Burgundy. I thanked him and took a sip before I offered, "Louise must have met someone, either in Toronto or in Newton, someone who had access to all this material."

I waited half-expecting him to fly at me even yet. "Perhaps we'll never know where they met, nor how they evolved the extortion scheme. Probably she was just sucked in by circumstances, by lack of money, lack of family, lack of direction—who knows? I don't see how we'll ever know, Joe, because Louise and Heather are gone."

It was a measure of our despairing intimacy that I called him Joe and he responded by saying, "I suppose you're right, Sydney. What's the good of speculating about reasons? She did it, and she died for it, and that's that."

A sudden, devastating thought had occurred to me. "Joe —Louise left me ten thousand dollars, which I assumed was a legacy from her aunt, invested wisely. But if she came back to Toronto, penniless, after her aunt died, then the money she left me must be blackmail money!"

He gave me a cynical look. "Don't give it another thought," he said. "That's probably no more crooked than most of the money floating about these days."

I paid him no attention. I could feel the heat rising to my temples. "I was actually contemplating taking a trip to Scotland with that money! Blood money."

He looked at me for a moment. "Well, you didn't know," he said practically.

"And now I do. I'll have to find a way to get it back to the people who paid, if I can find out which ones did."

There was a long, tired silence; then he offered reluctantly, "There's something I haven't told you. When Heather left—supposedly to take that traveling job—she asked me if I would pick up some of her mail from time to time and put it in our office safe. Two or three times I picked up packages from her post-office box, and twice from her rooming house."

"And you didn't wonder that she continued to get mail here in Toronto, if she was supposedly in Europe?"

He shrugged. "She asked me to do it," he said simply. "She knew she could trust me to lock the packages away until she came. I did wonder a little, since they were mailed from the United States, but I thought she might be mailing souvenirs to someone in the United States, then having them sent on here. I just didn't know why she was doing it, but frankly I didn't give it much thought. I knew she'd explain when she came back."

A little shadow crossed his face, and I put our mutual thought boldly into words. "Now that we know she isn't coming back, surely we can look into those parcels?"

He hesitated, then drained his glass. "All right. Let's go open them. Want another drink first?"

I shook my head. "No, thanks. Let's go."

We left the odor of stale beer and cigarette smoke and went out into the waning afternoon. A faint mist had dampened the cobblestones, and I thought worriedly that I must be on my way back to Newton before a crippling fog arrived.

In silence we climbed the steep little block to the deserted antique shop. "If anyone has been here," he said, "I hope my uncle never hears of it. If he had his way, we'd remain open twenty-four hours a day."

He unlocked the door and we went inside. The place smelled of old things, of silver polish and lemon oil and tattered satin and mellowed wood. I liked it. It was like the scent of Miss Grimes's little house, where everything gave off the odor of the past. I would have liked to stay here, shut in with the fragile lacy fans and the walleyed merry-go-round horse, away from the world. But that's nonsense,

I told myself sternly. Trouble came and found Joe Burnham here. We can't escape the world.

Soberly, Joe Burnham cleared some boxes of jewelry and old silver away from the front of the small safe, an ancient black affair with worn gold lettering on the front. He spun the dial, then twisted the steel bar, and opened the safe.

In the front there were several velvet trays of what appeared to be precious and semiprecious stones, many set in exquisite old settings.

To my glance of surprise, Joe Burnham said, "My uncle keeps this shop because he loves it, but he makes his real income buying and selling choice items to wealthy collectors."

From the back of the lower shelf, he pulled three tightly wrapped and sealed packages. "I picked up two of these from her post-office box, and one from her apartment house," he said. "She also left money so that I could pay her post-office-box rental."

He hesitated, his hands on the parcels. "I suppose we're justified in opening these, since she's—gone."

I nodded. "I think we have to open them, Joe, or we'll never know for sure."

He picked up a huge pair of library scissors and cut the heavy, knotted cord which bound the package. Then he sliced away at the tough strapping tape which further protected the parcel.

Inside was a blue zipper pouch, and when he unzipped this, we saw the money stuffed inside—a great stack of American tens and twenties.

"There must be two thousand here," he said drearily, and cut open the next package.

The second parcel appeared to contain about the same number of bills, and so did the third.

"God," he said grimly, and zipped up the pouches again. He thrust them, wrappings and all, back into the safe.

Then he sat down and looked at me. "Well, what are we

going to do?" he asked. "That money should go to the police in Newton. It's evidence."

"I know. But wait until they find Louise's murderer, if they ever do, and perhaps we can send the money back anonymously to the victims."

He cocked an eyebrow. "Why should you want to do that? Let the police handle it."

I shook my head stubbornly. "Not if there's any other way. All those people would be called in by the police. Why should they suffer anymore?"

He didn't argue. "Cup of tea?" he asked, in a surprisingly mundane manner, and put a battered kettle on the electric plate.

"Things are beginning to jell in my mind," he said. "Heather must have put as much money as she dared in her bank account in Newton, enough to call it insurance or a legacy from her aunt and uncle. The rest of her share, she simply mailed off to Toronto, in small, occasional packages. If one got lost, too bad, but there was nothing to connect Louise Albright with a packet of money addressed to Heather Smith in Toronto. And of course, there was more where that came from.

"Eventually, I suppose she'd have come back here and reclaimed it. In fact, the financial records you found at Mrs. Hungerford's must have been part of her first take. She must have driven up here, picked it up at the post office, and hidden it in her grandmother's basement. It was safe as houses there."

"Not from me," I put in mildly.

He nodded. "But you had a lead. Who else would have known about that package in your secret room? Not the police, certainly, and not her partner, presumably."

I wanted to assuage his hurt, even a little. I said, "Perhaps she planned to come back to Toronto to live, when she had saved as much as she wanted."

"Perhaps," he said quietly.

He poured the tea into beautiful bone-china cups. When

he saw my admiring glance, he said, "Uncle Horace believes in using beautiful things. We change from time to time, put others out in the shop. He says it keeps things beautiful, like wearing pearls to give them life."

Knowing the truth at last made me feel as though I'd been released from some terrible trap. I sank back in the chair and drank the excellent tea, while we discussed endlessly the incredible duality of Heather-Louise.

When at length I got up to leave, I said impulsively, "Joe, I'd like to buy that carrousel horse for my garden. How much is he, please?"

"I wish you'd let me give him to you," he said, as we walked out into the shop, "as a sort of gift from Heather. She was your friend, you know."

I was touched. "Thank you, Joe, but I'd rather pay for it, truly."

He loaded the wonderful old horse into my little car with some difficulty, and I waved at him as I drove away, back toward Newton and the people whose lives had touched Heather Smith's and her alter ego, Louise Albright.

## 21

*Defend us from all perils and dangers of this night.*
—Book of Common Prayer

When I drove into the dimly lit confines of Greenwood Place, I saw Domenic Lawrence's big Lincoln parked across the street from my rented house. He didn't see me at first, and his square, tanned face, in the glow of the streetlamp under which he sat, looked tired, a little grim, the eyes fixed on some distant vista.

While I hesitated, wondering what to say to him about Louise, he got out of his automobile and came over to mine.

"Well," he said, his hand on the door, whether to let me out or prevent me from leaving, I wasn't quite sure, "you are inclined to mystery, aren't you? I've been calling you, and no answer. No one seemed to know where you'd gotten to."

I wanted to snap back at him, he was so incredibly dictatorial, but I was too keenly aware of the blow I was about to deal him, and I muttered, "I've been to Toronto."

He looked faintly surprised. "Again? So soon?" Then, looking at the great-eyed horse, he said, "I see you've been shopping. Shall I take him inside for you?"

Carrying the horse, he followed me up the walk, past the dusty, tenacious chrysanthemums, to the front door of the little house.

When I opened it, Thomas, with one glad cry of relief, leaped onto my shoulder, thrust his face into mine, and sat there purring, looking like some fat-faced, happy Buddha. He regarded Domenic with a judicial eye, and Domenic scratched the cat's torn ear absently.

"Coffee?" I asked, and he agreed.

I led him into the sitting room and handed him a magazine, as though he were a patient in a dentist's waiting room. I was in a panic. What should I say to him? How could I tell him about Louise? I thought he might hate me forever, for destroying his illusions about the girl he'd loved—loves still, I corrected myself.

I opened the back door for Thomas, who streaked past me into the darkness, grateful for his release. Then I measured the coffee carefully into the pot and plugged it in to brew. I put cups and saucers and sugar and cream and crackers and cheese on the round, black-lacquered tray. But at last I could wait no longer. I must face Domenic and tell him what I'd learned.

When I went back into the sitting room, he was lolling there, his long legs stretched out to the gas log. I had a brief moment of seeing him vulnerable, his strong, tanned face looking young and boyish. He had nice eyebrows, thick and dark, with a humorous peak in the middle. I pictured him in law school, a handsome, breezy young man with a ready smile, and I thought that grief must have changed him, as it had changed me.

Revealing Louise's duplicity was bound to affect him, and I toyed with the idea of saying nothing about what I'd learned in Toronto.

No, it's no good. For a moment, I was afraid I'd spoken the words aloud, because he looked up at me inquiringly. "What is it?" he asked. "Something wrong?"

I hesitated. "Wait until we have our coffee, or would you like something stronger?"

He raised a quizzical eyebrow. "It must be something drastic. I assume you have something significant to tell?"

I found myself shaking violently, and suddenly the story I had to tell seemed wildly improbable, like something experienced in a dream, where someone you know suddenly becomes two persons, their personalities merging into each other. In the dream it is normal, accepted, but in real life terrifying and monstrous.

"I think I hear the coffee perking," I said, and fled into

the kitchen. I waited, leaning aimlessly against the counter, while the electric percolator burbled cheerfully, and then announced, with a final sigh, that the coffee was ready.

I carried the tray into the sitting room, and we drank the coffee, making small talk. And all the time I knew that he was studying me curiously, waiting for me to begin.

Finally I put my cup down and said, "I went to Toronto early this morning. I saw Joe Burnham again—the young man I told you about, the one who runs the antique shop where Heather Smith used to work."

His face was only mildly curious. "And?"

"I showed him some snapshots, some color prints, of Louise and her friends, at a party she gave several weeks ago. I wanted to see if he recognized anyone, because I believed Heather might be living in Newton."

His expression was dark now. "And did he?"

I watched his face as I said, "Louise was Heather Smith."

It was a long moment before comprehension set in. And then the anger swept his face. "Are you trying to say that Louise was blackmailing her friends?"

"It appears that way."

"What proof have you, what evidence?" But he knew it was true. He saw it in my face, in my tear-filled eyes.

Something in me stirred and lifted in pain, as I watched his face, and I wasn't quite sure whether it was remembered pain or the hurt of knowing that this man, to whom I was so strongly attracted, was emotionally wounded.

"I'm sorry," I said inadequately.

"Tell me," he demanded.

And so I told him the story Joe Burnham and I had pieced together, of a girl, Heather Louise Smith, who had her roots in Canada, but who apparently had been adopted by her Albright relatives in Chicago when her own parents died; a restless, rootless girl who had returned to her grandmother in Toronto, after the Chicago relatives died, and had set up a new life for herself.

He sat there silently, his big hands clasped loosely, as though the strength had gone out of them.

"But why?" he said finally. "What could have possessed her to take up this double life?"

"Money, I suppose. Joe Burnham said she loved beautiful things, but she lived in a shoddy apartment house, and there was no way out for her, or so she thought, not a fast enough way at least."

In the futile way of a woman, I poured more hot black coffee into his cup.

"Louise told me once that she had some musical training in Chicago," I said. "Presumably she wanted to continue her training and didn't have the money after her aunt and uncle died. Life in Toronto must have seemed like a dead end to her." Scrupulously I endeavored to fit myself inside the skin of a pretty, talented, penniless girl who saw nothing more exciting in her future than life in a dingy apartment house, listening to the dreary talk of Monica Kelly. Even marriage to Joe Burnham wouldn't have been enough. No, given a great hunger, a conviction that life should be full and exciting, a person like Heather-Louise might have been motivated to take a fast, easy, exciting way to acquire money.

"But why Newton?" he asked slowly. "I can understand her wanting to attend Hoffman Conservatory, but why would she return to her aunt's name and change her appearance, her whole identity?"

I waited for him to reach the same conclusion Joe Burnham and I had reached. "When she came here, she must already have decided to do this—this abominable thing."

"We feel that she must have had a partner," I said. "The blackmail money is still being collected, and I've had threatening phone calls from someone who apparently thinks I'm finding out too much."

He looked up quickly. "Why didn't you tell me that?"

I stared at him mutely, and he said flatly, "That can only mean you don't trust me."

I had the grace to blush. "I don't suppose I've trusted any- one lately."

"And now?" His gaze was very direct, and I wondered

why I had ever thought him anything but completely forth-right.

"Now," I said, "I know you're not Louise's partner."

His answer came like a shot. "And how do you know?"

I spread my hands helplessly. "I just know. Whoever it is must have hated Louise; you loved her."

His words, curiously, were almost the same as Joe Burnham's. "I loved Louise; I didn't know the other girl—Heather Smith."

He hesitated. "Oddly enough, I tried to ask you if you were involved in some sort of extortion scheme." He shot a look at my face. "Sorry. But turn about, you know. Cecily Andrews came to me recently for advice. Her ex-husband wants the little girl, you know."

I murmured, "Yes, I know, and I know she's being black-mailed."

"Well, then, can you blame me for wondering about you —an unknown quantity?"

"No," I said, "I suppose not. Is that why you invited me to lunch the day of the sidewalk art show?"

"Yes," he said, suddenly awkward, "that was partly it. But that was just an excuse, you know. I wanted your company."

I couldn't think of anything to say. I only knew that I felt deliriously happy for a moment.

He got to his feet. "Thank you for telling me everything. I'm going home and think this over."

"About the money Louise left," I said uncomfortably. "I don't want it, not now. Will you help me get it back to the people involved? I think a check from an attorney would be less frightening to them than a check from me."

He looked skeptical. "You'd do much better to tell Captain Morley and let him handle it."

I shook my head stubbornly. "I've been over that with Joe Burnham. It's not fair to get these people involved with the police. They've paid enough already."

He picked up his topcoat and put it on. "You're not really being fair, you know. All legalities aside, you're handicapping the police considerably by not giving them the true facts about Louise. There's a murderer running around loose, and the police haven't much to go on." He hesitated. "Hasn't it occurred to you that your own life must be in danger? The murderer knows you've been ferreting around; he knows you went to Toronto, and he undoubtedly fears that Louise herself told you something of significance, something which could trap him, sooner or later. He may feel he could get away with another seeming pot shot in the dark, or a small bomb in your car."

"I'll stay on lighted streets," I said firmly, "and I'll lock my car in the garage and always look under the hood before I start the engine."

He moved toward the door. "You're foolhardy," he said. "Let me tell Captain Morley what you've found out."

"No."

Exasperation and a certain grudging respect were written on his face. "Promise me you'll call me, or the police, if you get any more unpleasant phone calls or any unexpected visitors."

I hesitated, but that seemed reasonable enough. "All right. I promise. But I think I'm going back to California soon."

"Running away?"

"Call it that if you like," I said, nettled. "But since you've just pointed out to me the fact that I may be next in line for murder, you can scarcely blame me."

"No." He stood there, tall and overwhelmingly masculine in the little room. He hesitated, and started to leave. Then he came back to me. "Don't go," he said, and cupped my face between his two strong hands and kissed me.

I stood mutely, my own arms hanging awkwardly at my sides, palms in, like a young girl's. When Felix had kissed me, after so long a dearth of kisses, I'd felt flattered, perhaps even faintly titillated; but this was something else again. I was drowning in feeling, suffused with an emotion I'd thought long dead.

"Take care of yourself," he said gently, and was gone.

Only a stupid sense of pride kept me from running after him, from telling him to do as he liked about the police, at least so far as Louise was concerned. Suddenly I wanted him to make the decision. I wanted to lean for just a little against that tall, strong body, let the swift, stern mind take over the problem of Heather-Louise and her tidy little business. Like an orphan child, I suddenly became aware that I was completely alone in the world, and I was frightened.

I went to the front door and opened it, ready to call "Domenic!" but he was just pulling away, and my voice trailed off on the autumn wind.

Thomas came purposefully up the front walk, and I waited for him to come into the house. Then I made doubly sure that the front door was locked, and checked the catches on the long, narrow windows of the sitting room. Satisfied at last that the house was completely secure, I went into the kitchen to prepare my uninspiring supper of scrambled eggs, toast, and tea. With Thomas in mind, I dropped three brown-and-serve sausages into a little skillet, and soon had a tray ready to take back in before the fire.

While I ate and drank, I kept muddling things over in my tired brain. If they didn't find Louise's murderer soon, I would have to let the police know she'd been a blackmailer, even if I did it anonymously, for surely her death must be tied up with her crime.

When I'd tidied up after my solitary meal, I decided to chance a call to Cecily, although there was a strong likelihood she would be out with Lucien. I sorted out in my own mind the facts I could reveal to her and those I could not. Certainly I wasn't about to tell her that Louise was her blackmailer, but I could tell her that I had unearthed some of the money and that I wanted to return her share to her.

After the phone had rung a few times, her lazy drawl came over the wire. "Oh, Sydney. Where have you been? I tried to call you this afternoon. I'm having a little party here in my apartment. Come on over. They're all people from the conservatory, people you know."

"No, thanks," I said hastily. "I've been to Toronto, and I'm tired. It's a long drive."

I could feel the curiosity in her voice. "What is this with

you and Toronto? Do you have an exciting man hidden up there somewhere?"

I knew how dull I must sound. "Nothing like that. I was there on business."

I could almost see the disinterested shrug. "Oh, well, if you won't come. Sure now?"

"No, no, I couldn't, but thank you anyway."

She was about to hang up. "Cecily," I said, desperately. "Please listen to me for a moment. How much money have you paid out to the blackmailer?"

"Sydney, for heaven's sake!" She fairly hissed it at me. "There are two dozen people here. I can't talk about that now."

"Sorry. I have a reason for asking."

She calculated carelessly. "Oh, probably five hundred dollars. Why?"

I couldn't tell her that the legacy from Louise was like a heavy garment weighting my shoulders. "Some of the money has been recovered. I think you'll get yours back, Cecily."

I hung up quickly before she could ask any leading questions. I wanted desperately to get that ten thousand out of my possession and back to its rightful owners, as soon as it was legally possible. I was tempted to call Felix and Phil and Irene, but the likelihood was that they were at Cecily's party.

Perhaps it would be fair to pay five hundred to each of them. The chief difficulty, as I saw it, would be in finding out which of the people whose secrets were in the manila envelope had paid blackmail and were entitled to return of their money.

I thought of Tony Ferris and his little circle of Mafia types. The possibility that he had had Louise eliminated was a very distinct one, I thought, and I fastened on it with relief. If Tony Ferris had had her killed, then no one I knew and liked had done it.

Impulsively, I decided to sound him out about the money. He would be at the Ferris Wheel from now until closing, puffing his fat cigar, wandering among the tables, buying drinks for a favored few, eyeing the young girls.

I dialed the club and asked for Mr. Ferris. In a moment I heard his guttural accent. "Who'm I speaking to?"

"It's—well, never mind that," I said. "It's someone who knew Heather Smith."

The dark anger crackled in his voice. "I don't know no Heather Smith."

"I think you do," I said gently, and wondered why I had bothered to call him. If he had paid money to Louise, then it was dishonest money, anyway. It might better go to one of the others, to Phil and Irene, for instance, I decided ruthlessly.

"What do you want?" he demanded.

"I just wanted to return some money I think Heather borrowed from you, and I wanted to know the exact amount."

"I didn't lend your friend any money," he said. "I don't know what you're talking about." Then his voice hardened with renewed suspicion. "You're Louise's friend, the one who asked me about this Heather Smith. I know your voice."

I panicked then, and hung up quietly. I'd found out nothing, actually, except what I already knew: Tony Ferris was not the sort of man I wanted for an enemy. How foolish I'd been to call him! Yet I'd never thought he might recognize my voice. If he wanted to track me down, he could have someone at my door within the hour; I'd heard stories about Tony Ferris and the efficacy with which he dealt with people who crossed him.

I shook a little, half with laughter, half with fear. No one really wanted me to give that money back. "Better to let sleeping dogs lie." There was some truth in that, after all. These people had paid; they would be happy, naturally, to learn that Heather was dead; but they would want to forget the whole thing.

I rubbed my temples, which were throbbing painfully now. The best thing to do now was to go to bed and decide tomorrow what to do with my new-found knowledge and with Louise's money.

I went into the quiet kitchen, took two aspirin, and made myself a cup of tea, which I took back into the sitting room.

No reading tonight; my mind wouldn't stay focused long enough. I watched Thomas, who sat on top of the television set, assiduously cleaning his long white whiskers. In the tranquillity of the sheltered little street, I could hear every random leaf fall, every click of the branch outside the window, the branch that was a little too long, so that it scraped the window from time to time, like ghostly fingers.

I was afraid. With that awareness, came a realization: if I feared death, then I must want to live. Until now, I had searched for some clue to Louise's death, in anger and compassion, and with an intense feeling of curiosity. I had been fearless in my search, because I hadn't cared much what happened to me. Now, at last, I cared, and I asked myself why my own life had become precious to me once again. Was it because of the man who had walked out of here a little time ago, the man who had kissed me coolly and explicitly, and then walked away?

Whatever the reason, I could solve nothing tonight. In the morning, when my head was clear again, I'd face my new desire to live. Meantime, I might as well go to bed.

Despite a strong temptation to leave every light blazing, I turned off the sitting-room lights, turned off the comforting glow of the gas log, and went to peer out of the window. No moon sailed across that ink-black sky, and the pale street-lamps made only feeble inroads into the darkness. Greenwood Place, so close to the center of town, was cut off from traffic sounds, from traffic itself, by the insularity of its location and the sparsity of its houses. Once it had been a fashionable street, a street where the nouveau riche wanted to live and never stood a chance of finding a house. The carriages of the rich had once drawn up proudly before these doors, the breath of the horses showing white on the frosty air. The street had rung with the laughter of well-tended young people.

Now the half-dozen handsome houses were quiet specters of the past. One or two had been rented to young couples with a deep nostalgia for the past; the others, like Miss

Grimes's house, belonged to the solitary scions of the fine old families who had built them.

I knew my elderly neighbors only well enough to murmur to them, "Good morning." Tonight I could see that the corner house, occupied by a young married couple, was dark. They had waved at me, early that morning, when I was leaving for Toronto. Their own car had been packed to the doors with vacation luggage.

I dropped the heavy drapery into place, and the phone rang. I jumped nervously, then told myself heartily that it was only Cecily, who had no sense of time, anyway, calling me back to urge me to come to her party.

I picked up the receiver, and the unctuous voice said, "Sydney?"

I couldn't answer, and he laughed. "Come now, I know you're there."

Two can play at this, I thought, and hung up. In a moment, the telephone bell shrilled again imperiously, but I let it ring on and on.

It stopped finally, abruptly, as though an angry hand had slammed down the receiver. I stood there for several minutes, but it didn't ring again.

"Come on, Thomas," I said, merely to hear the sound of my own voice in the stillness. "Let's go upstairs."

Obediently he sprinted up the steps ahead of me. I had my foot on the bottom stair when I remembered my promise to Domenic. I had said I'd call either him or the police if I heard from my mysterious caller again.

I went back into the sitting room and switched on the little desk lamp. I picked up the receiver, but there was no dial tone. I clicked the little cross bar, but still nothing happened. Then I dialed the operator, but the phone was still dead. By now I was uneasy. Telephones did go dead, of course; there *was* trouble on this one sometimes; but I could think only that someone had cut the line outside the house. Had Tony Ferris, angered at my interference, sent one of his henchmen to silence me?

Oh, don't be ridiculous, I told myself bracingly. You're just a minor annoyance to a man like Tony Ferris. I turned out the lamp and started up the stairs again.

It was then that I heard the faint sound on the front porch, the merest scrape of a heel, perhaps. I halted, motionless, and so did Thomas. No one knocked at the door, and I was seized by the conviction that the person outside was the owner of the Voice on the telephone. That could only mean that he'd telephoned from the call box at the corner of Greenwood Place, and that he had walked or driven boldly down the street to my little house. I could not see him, yet I knew he was on the other side of that door.

Soundlessly, in my stocking feet, I went back into the sitting room and picked up the only weapon I could see, a wooden pestle resting in a mortar on the bookshelf. Then I followed Thomas into the dimly lit entry hall. He seemed to walk stealthily, on tiptoe, as cats do sometimes, and I watched him, hypnotized, as he moved to the front door. His head was tilted a little to one side, and he watched the door with visible caution and fear. He sensed, I knew, that unseen presence on the other side.

Then my heart gave a great lurch as I saw the knob turn; but the sturdy old door remained closed. Thomas' yellow fur began to bristle, and there was hatred in his yellow eyes, and in the flattening of his ears against his square head.

I picked up the cat and started up the stairs, clutching my foolish weapon in one hand. I wanted the safety of my bedroom, with its solid oak door and big brass bolt. There I could wait out the watcher until he went away, or until daybreak.

I had reached the second floor when I heard it—bold as brass, reckless, uncaring—the sound of a key being inserted in the big, old-fashioned lock.

The certainty of impending death came upon me then, and I began to tremble.

I went to the railing and looked down, down the thinly spiraling staircase, down into the dimly lit entry hall. It was a man, a dark-haired man in a belted raincoat. His head was bent, his hand on the light switch. And then the hall light went out, and I was alone, dreadfully alone in the threatening night, with all there was of evil just below me in the dark hallway.

I heard him mount the carpeted steps, his tread as measured and relentless as doom. My legs stiff and jerky with fear, I managed somehow to move silently, in my stocking feet, down the stairway toward the landing, toward safety. If I should meet him in the dark, I knew I would surely go insane with terror, but I kept moving, and arrived there before he reached the mirror.

Thomas, indignant at such rough handling, dashed back up the stairs, while I groped desperately for the catch. The door slid open. I fell inside and closed the door to the secret room, then sank gasping upon the floor of my sanctuary.

It seemed a mirage to me, a moment later, a figment of my fear-distorted mind, when I felt the panel swing in again, felt the breath of some fresher air in my nostrils. It was against all reason, yet I knew that someone had opened the door to the hidden room.

## 22

*Be able for thine enemy.*
—SHAKESPEARE

The truth came upon me then in a blinding flash. The creature, without form or substance, who stood there in the shapeless dark, could be only one person. For who, besides myself, had the key to the little house? Who, out of all the world, knew the secret of admittance to this little room?

The man, standing there so silently, waiting there, could be no one else but Miss Grimes's nephew.

Even while I crouched in the darkness, biting at my knuckles to keep from crying out, I found myself wanting to laugh, too, hysterically. One little sentence from Miss Grimes might have solved the whole thing: "My nephew's name is . . ."

At last he stirred, as though he had tired of playing cat-and-mouse with so stupid a victim.

"Sydney," he said gently, and this time I recognized his soft, warning voice, for there was no wall, no telephone, between us now.

He turned on the light and stood there surveying the room.

"I haven't been here for years," he remarked conversationally, his glance sweeping the small room. "I didn't quite make it the other night, while the concert was going on, although I had it in mind to search here before you came home. Actually, of course, I didn't believe Aunt Lucy had told you about this room. She never told anyone except family. She must have liked you."

His bright, interested eyes rested on my face.

"Paul Fleming," I said slowly. "You're Miss Grimes's nephew."

"Mmm."

How different he seemed to me now. The charming diffidence now seemed a kind of subtle malevolence, and the
bland, boyish face was the face of an unknown quantity.

"You never mentioned the fact that you knew this house,"
I said.

"Fortunately, the occasion did not arise. But would you
have suspected me, I wonder?"

I shook my head. "Not in the beginning, at least. There
would have been no reason. Except—" I stared at him.
"Your aunt predicted that you would come to a violent end."

I thought a faintly nettled look crossed his face. "Aunt
Lucy is a straitlaced old biddy."

He began to walk about, fingering things. "I wanted you
out of this house." Such venom lay beneath the calm words.

"But why?"

He looked at me speculatively, as-if to be certain I wasn't
dissembling. "I was pretty sure you didn't know, or you'd
have had the police on me long since."

"You mean know that you and Louise were partners in
blackmail?" I said, as calmly as though I'd known it all along.

He looked amused. "You may have found out about
Louise, but you didn't know I was her partner until I walked
in here, did you?"

"No," I said defiantly, "but I knew she had one. It was
you who tried to run me down in Toronto, wasn't it?"

"Yes," he said, almost absently. "It was I." He was looking about the little room, as though searching for something.
"I know she must have hidden it here. It's the logical place.

"Just as a matter of curiosity," Paul Fleming said pleasantly, "what did you find out in Toronto? I lost track of you,
you know, when you got on that ferry. I felt it wise to make
myself scarce then, because you would have seen and recognized me."

Perhaps, I thought desperately, I could keep him talking,
find a way out of this somehow. "I went to visit Heather
Smith's grandmother."

The look of amazement on his face was almost comical. "She had a grandmother?"

"Yes."

"And did you find out anything?"

I hesitated, then said boldly, "Yes, I found a large envelope full of material for extortion."

He frowned. "I knew she was mailing money off to Toronto, and occasionally going over there to deposit money in the bank, but I thought the material was here in this house."

He looked at me almost merrily. "I am to assume you know who Heather was?"

I looked straight at him, pretending to be unafraid. "Yes. I know that Heather and Louise were the same person."

"Well, it doesn't matter now. In any case, I need that money and material."

"So that you can continue your charming business, I suppose?"

He looked astounded. "Why not? It was my idea. Now that Louise is dead, everything is mine. I want the money, Sydney, and I want the clippings and other material."

I smiled nastily. "Since you're going to kill me anyway, at least allow me my small triumph. I'm not going to give them to you!"

I saw the mania then in his gray eyes, and knew that I was doomed. If for no other reason, he would kill me because I had dared to cross him, dared to interfere with his plans.

"Now, why should you imagine that I'm going to kill you? Just give me what is mine, and we'll both forget about this, Mrs. MacKenzie."

"Don't take me for an idiot," I said coldly.

The fury flicked across his handsome face, then was gone. "Never mind. I think I can find what I'm looking for; I've remembered something from my childhood. It's odd, you know, but when Louise was looking for a place to live, I saw your ad in the morning paper and sent her here." His tone was conversational, almost friendly. "Louise was very

modern in some ways, but I knew her fondness for antiques.
I told her about this room, and suggested she put the money
and material here. I assumed she did. I never dreamed she
took our . . . selling points . . . back to Toronto. But I suppose she thought it was safer, once she knew you'd learned
about this room."

He smiled and sat down on the old sofa. "Actually, I'd
half-forgotten this place myself," he said conversationally.
"I haven't been in this house for years."

And I know why, I thought, but I didn't answer him.

He began twisting the wooden scroll which decorated the
armrest of the old sofa, and suddenly it came out in his
hand, a long, narrow drawer with a small black leather notebook resting in it, and a thick packet of money which made
my eyes bulge.

"Clever, those early Americans," he drawled. "And very
clever of Louise to have spotted it. She must have seen one
somewhere."

I said dully, "She worked in an antique shop in Toronto."

He nodded approvingly. "She had good taste, Louise. Too
bad she didn't have good sense." He tucked the notebook in
his pocket and riffled the bills in satisfaction. "I knew she'd
hide some of it here," he said in satisfaction. "When we
planned the whole thing, we knew we'd have to be especially
careful, not to put too much in our bank accounts, and not
to be too showy in our style of living. We both diversified
our assets."

He tucked the money into another pocket. "This must be
from some of the really wealthy suckers. We split profits, of
course." He looked at me menacingly now. "But I know
there's more."

My teeth were chattering. "I'll take it to my grave, then."

"Brave words," he sneered. I could smell his expensive
soap and shaving lotion. It seemed to fill the tiny, airless
room, until I was sure that I would suffocate.

I looked at the small black leather notebook protruding
from his pocket, and against all reason, I was consumed by

curiosity. "What's in that notebook, to make it so important to you?"

"It wasn't just the notebook," he said absently. "It was the money, too. But most of the notes in that book are in my handwriting. When Louise and I first planned this, after we met in Toronto, I gave her this list of prospects to study, so that she could start working on information as soon as she moved to Newton." He smiled mischievously. "Now I would be too cautious to let my own handwriting appear on anything, but I was a bit of a novice when we started."

With amused deliberateness, he patted the notebook in his pocket. "It can't possibly matter to you, anyway, Sydney, so let's get on with the business at hand. Are you going to give me the papers you have?"

"My attorney has them," I said, lifting my head arrogantly.

"You mean Lawrence? I don't think so. He'd have told the police long since. He's a great believer in law and order. What were you saving them for, so you could capitalize on them yourself? Well, no matter. I'll find them after I've taken care of you. After all, I know this house well. I just need a little time to search."

Why do you want to kill me? I screamed silently, and he answered my unspoken question by saying, reproof in his voice, "If you had moved out of this house when I left that first note, you'd have saved yourself a good deal of trouble, and me, too. But now, as they say in the movies, you know far too much, Sydney."

I heard, then, the far-distant sound, the ringing of the front doorbell, and a sweet, desperate hope sprang up in me. But the ringing served only to bring Paul Fleming to a quick decision. He looked at me with malice.

"It's a bit late for callers," he said. "And in any case, it's far too late for you to have visitors, Sydney, my dear."

Every nerve in my body was straining at the leash, striving to communicate my predicament to that unknown person on the front porch.

Oh, please come in! I begged. Seek me, find me. Break down the front door and come find me!

But after a moment, the bell's insistent ring ceased, and the silence in the little room became something palpable. It stretched on and out, into forever.

The air now seemed lifeless and fetid, and my eyelids drooped with fatigue. An overwhelming, utterly foolish desire for sleep had seized me, and I no longer cared that Paul Fleming meant to kill me.

He bent over me, and I sat, limp as Raggedy Ann, on the old sofa. "Well, Sydney," he said, smiling ever so little. "Hail and farewell. I may have to leave your body here for a few days, until it's safe to remove it. But when you disappear, I imagine the police will feel certain you had something to do with Louise's murder, and that will be that. They won't search this house too thoroughly. They'll be sure you've run away, won't they?"

His thumbs were pressing on my windpipe now, and his handsome gray eyes were very close to mine. How smug and hateful his smile! Even with the blood beginning to pound in my eardrums, and the light in the small room becoming suffused with red, my memory picked out a sentence from Miss Grimes's description of her nephew: "He sat there, smiling . . . and I struck him."

On the couch beside me lay the wooden pestle from the sitting room. Somehow I picked it up, with fingers from which all feeling was fading. Somehow I brought it up against the back of that sleek brown head, and I struck as hard as I could.

And in some dim fastness of my brain, there was a bitter sort of exaltation at the buffeting of my enemy. This one is for Miss Grimes, I thought, and this one for me.

Paul fell back, stunned or dead, I knew not which, and I staggered to my feet, and stumbled to the door, which opened simply enough from within. My hand was on the latch, and the narrow door swung inward; but it was of no use. He was on his feet and after me again.

Who will take care of Thomas? I wondered, and that was my last thought, as I went whirling, twisting down some dark and fearsome corridor into safe nothingness.

## 23

*I do perceive here a divided duty.*
—SHAKESPEARE

How like a dream was life, now that it was drifting away from me. I had no wish to hold on to it. Soon I would be no longer Sydney, but someone infinitely wiser, infinitely happier. I let myself sink deeper into the pleasant abyss.

But someone was pulling me back into the world, someone's rough hands were drawing me into life. I opened my eyes.

I was lying on the landing, just outside the hidden room, and Domenic was kneeling beside me, the strangest expression on his tanned face. In the open doorway stood Captain Morley, looking very grim, as though there were something distasteful inside the room.

"Paul Fleming," I said weakly.

Domenic's voice was tight with anger. "We know," he said. "He tried to kill you."

"He . . . killed Louise," I said weakly.

I sensed the muscles in Captain Morley's body coiling themselves for action.

"God forgive me," said Domenic, "but I thought perhaps you had killed her."

"And for a time I thought you might have done it."

Thomas came and looked into my face, mewing inquiringly.

"He was sitting outside this door, you know," said Domenic, "looking into the mirror. That's how I found you. Animals see and hear things we cannot. He made it pretty obvious there was someone or something behind that looking glass, so I searched out the catch."

I could hear the sirens screaming, coming nearer and nearer, and I put my hand to my aching head, surprised to find my fingers shaking uncontrollably.

"Do you feel like going downstairs now?" Domenic asked, and I nodded.

He helped me to my feet and spoke briefly to Captain Morley. Paul, slouched on the old settee, was no longer smiling; yet there was no fear as yet on the smooth, handsome face.

He cast me a look of purest malevolence, and I turned my head away quickly and let Domenic lead me down the stairs.

With hands unexpectedly gentle, Domenic established me on the love seat and tucked Miss Grimes's hand-crocheted afghan around my feet. He looked about a bit wildly, as men generally do when confronted by a woman who is injured or ill.

"Now," he said briskly. "Would you like brandy?" He added, rather pathetically, "Is there brandy?"

I began to giggle weakly, and the pain in my throat made me cry, and he looked at me in horror.

"It's all right," I managed to gasp, still sobbing and laughing. "I'd like two aspirin and a cup of very hot tea. The tea bags are in a canister on the kitchen counter, and the aspirin is in the cupboard over the sink."

The doorbell rang, and Domenic went to answer it. I heard him speak briefly to the police officers before they went thumping up the stairs.

I lay on the love seat, fingering the little tufts on the woolly blue afghan, trying not to think, trying to forget my puffed and hurting throat.

Domenic brought the aspirin and ice water, which I gulped eagerly.

"I think perhaps a doctor should look at that throat," he said, adding grimly, "I'd like to get my hands on his throat for about five minutes."

I can scarcely deny that I experienced a little thrill of

pleasure at the tight anger in his tone. It made me feel like a weak, leaning sort of woman, cherished and protected.

"I'll be all right," I assured him. "I really don't need a doctor."

He brought the tea and stood watching while I drank it. He really was outrageously attractive, I thought, regarding through half-closed eyes his tall strength, and his mouth, so disciplined and finely cut, the square cut of his jaw.

"How did you and Captain Morley get here?" I asked.

He hesitated. "I decided to tell Morley the bare outlines of Louise's story. I'm sorry; I know you didn't want me to do it, but I have sworn to uphold the law, you know. I told him I had no idea who was being blackmailed, and I haven't."

I flung him a look of anger mixed with gratitude. "I'm sure he felt certain it was one of the blackmail victims who killed Louise. Don't you see that you put all those people in jeopardy?"

He shrugged. "It was either they or you."

I could feel my cold cheeks growing warm, but I didn't ask what he meant.

"I called you from Morley's office to tell you what I'd done, and ask if you'd talk to him tomorrow. The operator said the line was out of order. I didn't like that much, with you alone in the house, so we drove on over. You didn't answer the bell, and by then we were really alarmed, so I broke a window and entered."

I tried to smile. "Thank God."

Surprisingly he grinned. "And thank that yellow tomcat. I've always considered dogs far more intelligent than cats, but I must admit your cat came as close to telling us where you were as an animal could."

The men were coming down the stairs now. Captain Morley entered the sitting room to ask, "Are you all right, Miss Webster? We can take you down and let the police surgeon have a look at you."

"No, no, I'm all right, truly," I said.

His glance flicked from me to Domenic and back again. "In that case," he said, "we'll be getting on. I won't bother you for a statement until tomorrow."

They went out, and the heavy front door banged after them, and then I heard the motor of the police car sighing away into the quiet night.

Throwing aside the afghan, I struggled to my feet, then sat down again abruptly. My legs were unbelievably wobbly.

"What are you doing?" Domenic demanded.

"There's something I must get."

"Then I'll get it for you."

I sank back on the sofa. "In the little room, the secret room," I said, "underneath the bottom of that old chair, you'll find a large manila envelope. Would you bring it to me?"

He was back in a few moments. He handed me the envelope silently.

Weighing it in my two hands, I tried to think of what was right, what was legal and ethical; but I could only remember the people who had paid and paid again for their transgressions: people like Irene and Phil, and Cecily and her small daughter. Their precarious happiness could be destroyed so easily. . . .

While Domenic watched, unspeaking, I leaned forward and laid the envelope on the grate. The gas flames licked away slowly and steadily, and finally consumed the papers in one last gulp of blazing orange.

## 24

*And love-lamps in the casement hung.*
—THACKERAY

We sat opposite each other, Domenic and I, on either side of the brown-marble fireplace. Scarcely twenty-four hours had passed, yet everything was changed now. The little house was warm and friendly again, sheltering us against the wild October night.

We drank coffee laced with the last of the Drambuie, as though this were a celebration of some sort, and perhaps it was, in a way. Thomas, very graceful, very alert, very dignified, as befitted one who had saved his mistress's life, sat erectly before the blue and yellow flame.

All about us were the things I cherished as though they were my own: the carved ivory chessmen, waiting silently on their squares of dark and light; the desk, with graceful, curving legs; the shimmering green of the faience cat who guarded the fireplace; the framed sampler, its straggling cross-stitched letters saying, "God Bless Our Home"; the blue-sprigged potpourri jar, casting a faint scent of musk rose on the air. Beautiful things, the sort of things for which Heather had been willing to sell her soul.

"Louise loved these things," I said.

Domenic nodded, as though he had followed my thought. "I think perhaps she found a security in beautiful things which she did not find in people."

Holding my cup in my two hands, I leaned my head back against the chair. "I've been trying to piece it all together," I said. "I know, of course, that Paul Fleming finally admitted to Captain Morley that he did kill Louise."

"Yes. Because she had made up her mind to give up their

dirty little business, and to send all the incriminating evidence back to the people concerned."

I looked at him. "That was because of you," I said quietly. "She did love you. She was going to give it up for you."

"Perhaps." He sounded remote. "At any rate, Fleming wasn't about to give up his tidy little unearned increment. He wanted to add new clients, in fact. But equally important, Louise threatened to expose Fleming to Barbara Carmichael unless he broke his engagement to her. Apparently Louise couldn't see letting that lovely, sweet girl marry a man like Paul Fleming.

"That did it. I don't think Fleming loves Barbara; I don't think he has ever loved anyone. But she is eminently suitable to be the wife of an up-and-coming composer-conductor. Barbara is rich, and her family is very influential."

"Poor Barbara," I said feelingly, and lapsed into silence. I knew too well the shattering blow which had been dealt today to that sheltered young woman.

I asked finally, "How did he accomplish killing Louise so neatly and so quietly?"

"Apparently he and Louise had arranged to meet in the park that night, ostensibly to discuss breaking up their little business. But actually he planned to kill her, of course. He got there a few minutes before she did, waited in the bushes, and shot her. Then he calmly hid the gun in his car, went back, and picked up Barbara, as though nothing had happened. To explain the delay, he told Barbara his car wouldn't start, and they walked through the park and found Louise. It was sheer, cold-blooded nerve on his part."

I shivered.

"Well," he said tiredly, "you'll have to give him A for unmitigated audacity. He deliberately took Barbara through that park, so they'd find Louise's body. It was a bold stroke, but it worked. No one suspected those two, so young and clean and above suspicion. And of course no one dreamed of any connection between Fleming and Louise; they'd never been seen together. So far as anyone knew, they hadn't met, beyond some casual greeting at the conservatory."

I went over and took the china dog from the whatnot stand and sat fingering it. "Strange how his aunt recognized that he was sadistic and even dangerous. She said he would come to a violent end, and he will, unless they prove him insane."

Domenic laughed bitterly. "He is, I should say, ultrasane. He's completely, utterly rational, with no human feelings, so far as I can see. The trouble is, he's a good actor; he can turn on charm and diffidence as though they came from a vending machine. Believe it or not, he had the gall to ask if I'd represent him!"

There was a strange, comfortable little silence; then I asked, almost languidly, "Did Paul tell you how he came to meet Louise and plan this thing?"

He said grimly, "I believe they had to prod his memory a little, but he finally told. He met Louise when he was vacationing in Canada a couple of years ago. She was Heather Smith then, of course. Apparently they had some sort of brief romance, and he finally confided his scheme to her. She was made to order for the job. She had no family ties—she apparently didn't count the senile old grandmother." His face darkened. "I suppose they recognized some sort of avariciousness in each other, some abnormality of character which made them capable of doing what they did for money."

I looked at him mutely, feeling his pain and his disillusionment as though they were my own.

"He gave her that notebook full of potential victims, with notes on possible points of attack. Then they planned their strategy. Louise was honestly a music student. Fleming lent her the first semester's tuition, and she enrolled at Hoffman under the name given her by her foster parents, using her middle name, Louise, instead of Heather, which was too distinctive. Then she became Louise Albright, and quite legitimately so."

He stared into the glowing gas log, sorting out, I supposed, the pieces of the puzzle.

"Heather knew very few people in Toronto. She told them

she was going to Europe. Then she went back over the border to the United States, of which she was a citizen, in any case. She'd opened a couple of bank accounts in Toronto, and had rented a post-office box and arranged with Joe Burnham to pick up any packages which arrived for her, and put them in his safe. Everything was covered, I think, every eventuality, in a very practical, commonsense sort of way."

I felt a certain twinge of admiration for this daring girl who had seized life by the throat and had shaken what she wanted out of it.

Domenic went on, as though the story he was telling were about someone remote, someone he hardly knew, and indeed, that was the case, I suppose.

"She came to Newton, enrolled at Hoffman, and settled down to making a new life and personality for herself. She made lots of friends; she was invaluable to Fleming, as he had known she would be, in ferreting out bits of information about people. That photograph of Tony Ferris with the Mafia man, for instance—Louise took that one night at the Ferris Wheel, and Tony never even suspected. The evening job at the Ferris Wheel, incidentally, was a great source of information for them. And as Fleming said, it amused her to blackmail Tony, with him not suspecting her in the slightest. After all, he wasn't exactly lily white."

I said, marveling, "And she really became a different person, writing with her right hand instead of her left, changing the color of her hair, changing her name. More coffee, Domenic?"

"Please, Sydney." He made the name, my father's name, which I'd never liked, sound so completely feminine that I found it pleasant at last.

I said, "I remember someone saying, in *The Thirty-nine Steps,* that the way to assume a new identity is to *be* the person, and forget that another self ever existed. If you do that, you don't need a disguise. And of course Louise did just that. When she was Heather, she was Heather and no one else; when she became Louise again, she put away the memory of Heather."

After a little I said, "I can see that Paul Fleming is a sort of perverted genius. I suppose the only reason he let Louise hang onto that envelope of pictures and clippings was so that he'd have no evidence at all in his possession, in the very unlikely event that they were ever caught."

Domenic smiled in grim satisfaction. "He slipped up on one thing, though. He'd forgotten all about that little leather notebook with the list of names, had in fact assumed that Louise had destroyed it. When she told him she wanted to dissolve their partnership, he threatened to expose her, although of course he wouldn't have dared. She countered with the fact that she still had the notebook and would show it to Barbara. I suppose she signed her death warrant right then. Fleming was not about to put up with any sort of interference with his plans. He intended to live comfortably now, then marry Barbara Carmichael and live even more comfortably. Louise got in the way of his life plan, and he eliminated her. To him it was as simple as that. Morley told me that Fleming shows no remorse, only anger and impatience because his plans have gone awry."

"I know," I said dreamily. "My landlady, Miss Grimes, is his aunt, you know, and she said he was sadistic." Then I added in dismay, "Oh, poor old thing. How dreadful this will be for her, even though she expected him to come to some bad end. She's such a dear. I wish she didn't have to know."

I thought of Miss Grimes in her sensible shoes, and her frankly white hair, such a rarity in these days of easy hair coloring. My heart sank at the idea of letting her know that her prophecy had come true, for I knew that she had loved Paul Fleming when he was a small boy.

Domenic stood up. "Well, it's over now, and I'd better be going. You should be getting some sleep. You've had a nasty shock. Why don't you ask Cecily or Irene to stay with you for a night or two?"

I shook my head. "The danger's past. And I'm a loner."

He regarded me thoughtfully. "I wonder."

To my intense horror, I felt a slow blush spreading from

my neck straight up to my forehead. To change the subject, I asked quickly, "Why was Paul Fleming after me, right from the beginning? Those notes I found—"

"He says quite frankly that he wishes he'd killed you; then he might not be in this predicament. At first he meant only to frighten you away from this house. He wanted that notebook and any money Louise might have left. Also, he thought the blackmail documents were hidden here, and felt it was only a question of time until you found them.

"Then, when you went off to Toronto the first time, he knew you were on the trail. He was waiting at the motel and decided to eliminate you."

Domenic regarded me coldly. "You are a bit of an idiot, you know, running off to Toronto on your own, not once but twice. What if Burnham had been the killer? What if Fleming had been a bit quicker that night?"

I shuddered, and he added more gently, "It's all over now. The bad is all behind you."

"Yes," I said slowly, "I think it is, at last."

And over for the others, I hoped, for all the people who had been bled dry by Paul Fleming and by the girl who had been so truly a split personality: Heather-Louise, who had been ruthless with some, but kind to me, and who had loved Domenic enough to give up her lucrative racket and, thereby, her life.

Irene and Phil could have their baby now, without too much fear of exposure, and perhaps someday things would work out for them, so they could be married. Cecily would leave Lucien and go to New York to find whatever it was she was seeking. She would always "land in a butter-tub," as my grandmother would have put it. Lucien would be hurt, but in any case, Cecily was bad for him. He had talent; he'd be all right eventually.

Now Felix could live as he liked to live, graciously and comfortably. Perhaps he might even marry one day, although I rather doubted it. The role of perennial bachelor suited him very well. Certainly he didn't appear heartbroken over Louise's death. He had been attracted to her, I thought, but he hadn't really loved her.

As for Tony Ferris, I thought grimly, perhaps I should have mailed that photograph to the police. The sooner he was tripped up, the better. He was, in his crude way, a sinister man.

I looked up at Domenic. "Why do you suppose she left her money to me? I wish I could understand how her mind worked."

He shrugged. "I suppose it was mainly to assuage her guilt. And she liked you, you know."

I sighed softly. "And I liked her. Isn't it a pity? She had everything: looks and intelligence and some musical gift, and she threw it all away, just to make some quick, easy money."

"Oh, I think it was more than that," Domenic said, staring off into space. "I think it was the challenge of the game, as much as anything. Louise liked a dare."

"Yes."

"Now I really must go." He took my hand. It was something more than a handshake, something less than a caress. I felt my own hands, slim and helpless, trembling a little in his strong clasp. His grip became tighter.

"I'll call you tomorrow," he said. "Will that be too soon?"

I shook my head, speechless as a young girl. "It's not too soon," I said. "I'll wait for your call."

He went then, leaving me sitting in the big wing chair before the gas fire in Miss Grimes's Victorian sitting room. But it was all right. I knew he'd be back tomorrow.

*Foreboding mansions,
moonlight and the moaning wind
. . . a setting for romance,
intrigue and the supernatural*

# GOTHIC MYSTERIES

| | | |
|---|---|---|
| **BELLWOOD** *Elisabeth Ogilvie* | | 60c |
| **THE BRIDE OF MOAT HOUSE** | *Peter Curtis* | 60c |
| **CHATEAU IN THE SHADOWS** | *Susan Marvin* | 60c |
| **COME TO CASTLEMOOR** *Beatrice Parker* | | 75c |
| **THE CRAIGSHAW CURSE** *Jean Francis Webb* | | 60c |
| **THE DANCER'S DAUGHTER** | *Josephine Edgar* | 60c |
| **DUNSAN HOUSE** *Anita Grace* | | 60c |
| **GIANT'S BREAD** *Mary Westmacott* | | 60c |
| **THE HERMITAGE** *Mary Kay Simmons* | | 75c |
| **A HOWLING IN THE WOODS** | *Velda Johnston* | 60c |
| **I START COUNTING** *Audrey Erskine Lindop* | | 75c |
| **THE JACKAL'S HEAD** *Elizabeth Peters* | | 75c |
| **THE SANDALWOOD FAN** | *Katherine Wigmore Eyre* | 75c |
| **TIMBALIER** *Clayton W. Coleman* | | 60c |
| **WOMAN IN THE MAZE** *Maeva Park Dobner* | | 60c |

## DELL BOOKS

*Biggest dictionary value*
*ever offered in paperback!*

---

The Dell paperback edition of

# THE AMERICAN HERITAGE DICTIONARY
## OF THE ENGLISH LANGUAGE

- Largest number of entries—55,000
- 832 pages—nearly 300 illustrations
- The only paperback dictionary with photographs

---

**These special features make this new, modern dictionary clearly superior to any comparable paperback dictionary:**

- More entries and more illustrations than any other paperback dictionary
- The first paperback dictionary with photographs
- Words defined in modern-day language that is clear and precise
- Over one hundred notes on usage with more factual information than any comparable paperback dictionary
- Unique appendix of Indo-European roots
- Authoritative definitions of new words from science and technology
- More than one hundred illustrative quotations from Shakespeare to Salinger, Spenser to Sontag
- Hundreds of geographic and biographical entries
- Pictures of all the Presidents of the United States
- Locator maps for all the countries of the world

## A DELL BOOK 75c

*Novels of Romance and Chilling Suspense . . .*

# GOTHIC MYSTERIES

by

## Mary Roberts Rinehart

### DELL BOOKS

If you cannot obtain copies of these titles from your local bookseller, just send the price (plus 15c per copy for handling and postage) to Dell Books, Post Office Box 1000, Pinebrook, N. J. 07058. No postage or handling charge is required on any order of five or more books.